Wounded Prey

"We looked back and saw people being stabbed and scalped," Lydia said. "Women and men were bleeding. Children screaming. Didn't you hear it, Mr. Slocum?"

"I was tracking a wounded elk," he told them. "You're lucky I found you. This is wilderness."

"Can you take us back there, see if anybody's still alive?" Jasmine asked.

Slocum thought about it for a long moment. If what the women had told him was true, a wagon train had been attacked by Indians and white men. People had died. They hadn't used guns, which meant whoever committed that atrocity knew they had the upper hand. They knew they were attacking helpless people, people who wouldn't resist. Why? To rob them, probably. And, if his hunch was right, to leave no witnesses.

JAKE LOGAN

SLOCUM
AND THE
BIG TIMBER BELLES

JOVE BOOKS, NEW YORK

THE BERKLEY PUBLISHING GROUP
Published by the Penguin Group
Penguin Group (USA) Inc.
375 Hudson Street, New York, New York 10014, USA
Penguin Group (Canada), 90 Eglinton Avenue East, Suite 700, Toronto, Ontario M4P 2Y3, Canada
(a division of Pearson Penguin Canada Inc.)
Penguin Books Ltd., 80 Strand, London WC2R 0RL, England
Penguin Group Ireland, 25 St. Stephen's Green, Dublin 2, Ireland (a division of Penguin Books Ltd.)
Penguin Group (Australia), 250 Camberwell Road, Camberwell, Victoria 3124, Australia
(a division of Pearson Australia Group Pty. Ltd.)
Penguin Books India Pvt. Ltd., 11 Community Centre, Panchsheel Park, New Delhi—110 017, India
Penguin Group (NZ), 67 Apollo Drive, Rosedale, Auckland 0632, New Zealand
(a division of Pearson New Zealand Ltd.)
Penguin Books (South Africa) (Pty.) Ltd., 24 Sturdee Avenue, Rosebank, Johannesburg 2196,
South Africa

Penguin Books Ltd., Registered Offices: 80 Strand, London WC2R 0RL, England

This is a work of fiction. Names, characters, places, and incidents either are the product of the author's imagination or are used fictitiously, and any resemblance to actual persons, living or dead, business establishments, events, or locales is entirely coincidental.

SLOCUM AND THE BIG TIMBER BELLES

A Jove Book / published by arrangement with the author

PRINTING HISTORY
Jove edition / July 2011

ISBN: 978-0-515-14963-0

JOVE®
Jove Books are published by The Berkley Publishing Group,
a division of Penguin Group (USA) Inc.
375 Hudson Street, New York, New York 10014.
JOVE® is a registered trademark of Penguin Group (USA) Inc.
The "J" design is a trademark of Penguin Group (USA) Inc.

PRINTED IN THE UNITED STATES OF AMERICA

10 9 8 7 6 5 4 3 2 1

1

John Slocum ground his teeth down to keep from cussing the kid. He wanted to drive a fist into his face and mash that idiotic smile to a pulp. The kid had the brains of a field mouse as far as Slocum was concerned. He hadn't wanted to bring him along on the elk hunt, but the owner of the hotel had insisted.

"Donnie's a good kid. I want you to teach him how to hunt," Ray Mallory had said. "He's big enough now."

"Has he ever hunted before?" Slocum asked.

"Rabbits and squirrels."

"Hunting elk is a pretty big step up," Slocum had said. "Didn't he ever bring down a mulie or an antelope?"

"Nope. Nobody hereabouts would ever take him hunting, so he never learned."

"Why wouldn't they take him?" Slocum had all kinds of warning bells ringing in his mind, and some of them gonged as loud as a brass bell.

"Well, Donnie's a little slow. His ma died when he was still in short britches and I been busy with the hotel."

1

"Do you hunt yourself, Mr. Mallory?" Slocum asked the hotel owner.

Mallory shook his head.

"I never shot a gun in my life."

"That's just dandy, Mr. Mallory."

"I'll pay you extry, of course."

"How much extra?"

"Why, I don't know. A sawbuck maybe."

"Make it a double sawbuck and I'll take little Donnie with me up into the high country, teach him how to call an elk in close and drop it with a single shot."

Mallory had beamed under his full beard flanked by ornate muttonchops.

"Done," Mallory had said, and Slocum had taken the kid and two pack mules out of Big Timber and into the Absarokas, where the elk had returned that Montana spring.

Now, the kid had wounded a big cow elk, gut-shot it, and Slocum had to track it through rough country, down a steep slope, over rocks and deadfalls, patches of snow that still lingered like scraps of icy antimacassars.

"I'm real sorry, Mr. Slocum," Donnie said. He gripped the single-shot .30 caliber Remington as if it were a stick of wood. The kid was still shaking. He had been shaking with buck fever when Slocum told him to take the shot.

"You stay here with the horses and the pack mules, Donnie," Slocum said. "Don't move until I get back."

"Where you goin'?" Donnie asked.

"You wounded that cow elk. I have to track her and put her down."

"I'm plumb scared to be up here all by myself."

"Well, I'm not taking you and the pack mules down that slope until I've taken care of that wounded cow. You just have to stay here."

"Don't be gone too long," Donnie said, his voice quavering. His hands still trembled as if he had a case of the ague.

"And don't you put another bullet in that rifle," Slocum said.

He looked at the kid one last time, debating whether or not he should hit him with his fist or lay him over his knee and spank him.

"Don't shoot anything," Slocum said. "Even if a bear comes at you growling and snarling."

"A bear?"

"They're out of hibernation by now, and some of the females may have cubs. If one sees you, she may come after you and tear you apart limb by limb."

"Christ," Donnie said.

"Don't take the name of the Lord in vain, kid, or I might tear you apart."

"Yes, sir," Donnie said, his voice pitched to a high tremolo.

"Best you walk back up where we left our horses and the pack animals. Just stay there until I get back. You can stay out of the sun in that little cave in the bluff."

"Yes, sir," Donnie said.

"Make sure there's no bear in the cave before you crawl in."

The boy choked up with emotion. Slocum suppressed a smile as he turned away.

Slocum gained some satisfaction by scaring the kid half to death before he started walking to the place where the cow elk had been shot. It stood fifty yards downslope, where a blue spruce was sheltering a circle of unmelted snow.

There was a clear blood trail. The cow had turned after it had been shot and run straight downhill. Slocum saw bits of lung matter mixed in with the blood. It was worse than he had thought. The elk hadn't been gut-shot. The kid had hit the cow in the chest or neck. There were more scraps of the white rubbery substance.

"He either hit it in the windpipe or the lung," Slocum said to himself as he grabbed a limb and let himself slide over a steep piece of ground. There was no telling how badly the cow had been hit, but there were streaks of blood along the ground torn up by the elk's hooves.

The elk changed course a hundred yards farther on, angling left along a small ridge. Flecks of blood marked its passing, and there were more than a few overturned rocks and small stones. The tracks were easy to follow, but Slocum was surprised at the distance the cow had covered after being hit by a .30 caliber lead slug.

The tracks led around a large boulder sunk into the mountainside. Then the elk had turned again and headed straight down through treacherous brush and mounds of rocks. It was rough going and Slocum was glad he had on hunting boots and not his riding boots. More than once he had to grab a sapling to keep from falling or tumbling headlong into an overgrown ravine.

He finally reached the bottom of the steep slope and saw the tracks and blood spots leading off toward a creek. There was no more windpipe or lung material and no streaks of blood. Just drops of blood that were still wet.

The elk had gone into the creek and waded across. Slocum found a place where there were rocks he could use for stepping-stones. He crossed the creek, but at the edge of the farther bank, his boot slipped off the rock and he stepped into icy cold water. He flopped up on the shore and walked back to where the elk tracks emerged from the creek.

He followed these for a hundred yards or so, and realized that the cold creek water must have closed the wound in the elk's chest. Cauterized it with ice-cold water. He found other tracks and studied them for several moments. The wounded elk had joined a small herd and they had all moved off through the timber. He could no longer distinguish the wounded elk's tracks from the others.

He stopped and leaned against a tall, thick pine tree. He reached into his shirt pocket and pulled out a cheroot. He put it in his mouth, but didn't light it. He knew he would never find the elk now. The tracks led straight up into thick timber and rocky outcroppings. It would take more time than he had to spare. The kid was back up there with their horses and the pack mules, probably pissing his pants by now.

Slocum waited a few moments until his breathing returned to normal, then started back toward the creek.

That was when he heard an odd sound. He stopped and turned his head. There it was again. It was a soft groaning sound. He cupped a hand to his ear. It was more like moaning or whimpering. Human, not animal.

He stepped slowly and carefully toward the sound. It was downstream from where he had crossed the creek. As he walked, he saw a logging road on the other side of the creek. The road ended in a wide, circular turnaround.

The sounds grew louder as he approached a small bluff. Large outcroppings of boulders loomed in the brush like the remnants of ancient buildings or monuments. He put a thumb on the hammer of his Winchester and continued on.

He rounded one of the boulders and saw that there was a cave at the base of the limestone bluff.

He heard the unmistakable sound of a woman crying. Then there was another sound, a whimpering, sobbing sound that also seemed to be female.

Slocum slid forward until he was right next to the cave.

"Who's in there?" he called.

The sobbing and the crying ceased.

"I got a gun," a man's voice said. "I'll shoot if you come in."

"Hold on," Slocum said, lowering his voice. "I'm just a hunter passing by. Anybody hurt in there?"

"You ain't no Injun?" the man said.

"No. I pass for a white man in most circles."

He heard a rustling in the cave. A man's head poked out and looked at him. Then it disappeared.

"We ain't hurt, but we're mighty scared," the man said.

"Come on out," Slocum said. "It's safe."

A small wizened man wearing a dark suit that was covered with dust, a string tie, and a grimy white shirt stepped from the cave. He was followed by two of the prettiest women he had ever seen. Their eyes were wide, and much of the color had drained from their faces.

"Who are you?" one of the women said to him.

"I'm John Slocum, ma'am," he said, and doffed his hat.

"No," the woman said, "you're a god. You're our savior."

Slocum smiled.

"If you say so," he said, holding out a hand to help her emerge from the cave.

The creek gurgled as it surged past, and sunlight danced on the waters. Little flecks of gold sparkled in its depths, and a blue jay flitted in the aspens and pines, as curious as Slocum about the strange assemblage at the mouth of the cave.

2

Slocum helped the younger woman exit from the cave. When they stood close to each other, the women looked almost like sisters. But he could see that one was quite a bit older than the other. Both were very beautiful.

The man dusted himself off. He slapped and rubbed his hands over his suit. Then he looked up at Slocum and cocked his hatless head.

"Mister, I'm sure glad you come along. I thought we were all going to die in that filthy little cave."

"Who are you?" Slocum asked. "And what were you doing in that cave?"

"I'm Leroy Fenster of Saint Louis, although we came here by way of San Francisco. These are my dear clients, mother and daughter, Jasmine Lorraine and her daughter, Lydia. The Lorraine Sisters. Ever heard of 'em?"

Slocum shook his head.

"Nope," he said. "Can't say as I have." He took the cheroot from his mouth and slipped it back in his pocket.

"They're singers," Fenster said. "Known all over the West. Or soon will be."

7

"You haven't answered my question, Mr. Fenster," Slocum said. "What in hell were you three doing hiding out in a cave way up here in the timber?"

"Ah," Fenster said, "it's a long story. We were—"

"We were traveling by stagecoach with a wagon train," Jasmine interrupted, pushing Fenster aside. She was taller than he was and, for Slocum's money, had a lot more charm and gumption than the odd-looking little man. "We're supposed to be in Big Timber, Montana, by tomorrow. A bunch of outlaws and Indians attacked us this morning. I think the wagon master made a wrong turn or else he was in cahoots with those—those savages."

"That's right," Lydia said. She stepped close to her mother and looked up at Slocum. Both women had blue eyes and strawberry hair that reached almost to their waists. Their tresses were shiny and the sun turned them golden. They had small waists and wore traveling skirts and boots, and matching blouses with the initial *L* embroidered above the left pockets. They wore soft red lipstick and their fair cheeks had been brushed with a delicate rouge. Slocum could smell their perfume, the scent of lilacs, he thought.

"If Mama hadn't grabbed my hand and gotten me and Mr. Fenster out of the coach, we'd all be dead by now. It was horrible. The Indians shot arrows, and the white men used knives to kill our traveling companions."

"What?" Slocum said. "You were on a stage and it got robbed?"

"They swooped down on us," Jasmine said. "Out of nowhere. There were two wagons. We were in the coach, right behind the lead wagon. In the confusion, I got my daughter and Mr. Fenster out one of the doors and we ran and ran up this road, jumped across the creek, and hid in this cave."

"We looked back and saw people being stabbed and scalped," Lydia said. "Women and men were bleeding. Children screaming. Didn't you hear it, Mr. Slocum?"

He explained to them where he had been and pointed to the opposite slope.

"I was tracking a wounded elk," he told them. "You're lucky I found you. This is wilderness."

"You can say that again," Fenster said, his brown eyes like a pair of polished buttons.

"We left all those people down there on the road," Jasmine said.

"And all our things are still there," Lydia added.

"Where?" Slocum asked.

Jasmine pointed down the road, which was littered with pine bark and branches, the detritus left behind by wood-cutters who hauled timber out of the mountains and down to the sawmills.

"Can you take us there, see if anybody's still alive?" Jasmine asked.

Slocum thought about it for a long moment. If what the women had told him was true, a wagon train had been at-tacked by Indians and white men. People had died. They hadn't used guns, which meant whoever committed that atrocity knew they had the upper hand. They knew they were attacking helpless people, people who wouldn't resist. Why? To rob them, probably. And if his hunch was right, to leave no witnesses.

"You'd better all stay here," Slocum said. "I'll walk down there and look things over."

He pointed up to the opposite slope.

"I've got a boy up there on that mountain," he said. "He's waiting for me. We have two horses and two pack mules. After I check things out where you say you were attacked, I'll go up there and we'll ride back down here."

"What if those Indians and those men are still looking for us?" Jasmine asked. "They'll murder us while you're gone."

Slocum unbuckled his gun belt.

"Any of you know how to shoot a pistol? This is a Colt 45, double-action revolver."

"I—I do," Jasmine stammered. "I mean I fired my father's pistol a few times. I don't think it was that big."

"You just thumb back the hammer, aim, and shoot," Slocum said, handing her the gun belt. If you see sign of any of those robbers, you just shoot it twice and I'll get here as fast as I can. Okay?"

"Okay," Jasmine said. She held the gun belt in her hands as if it were a dead snake. Or a live one. Lydia eyed it and took a step backward.

"A gun's just a tool, ma'am," Slocum said. "It can give a warning or it can drop a man at close range. Take the pistol in your hand. Get used to it. Use it if you have to. As a warning or as a weapon."

"I—I'll try," Jasmine said. She pulled the pistol from its holster. Her hand dropped with the weight, but she brought it back up and put her finger inside the trigger guard and clasped the grip with her hand.

"It's a lot heavier than my daddy's pistol," she said. "But his gun was like this. You had to pull the hammer back each time you shot it."

"Well, then," Slocum said. "You're halfway there, Miss Jasmine. It is Miss, isn't it?"

"Yes. I'm not married."

"Neither am I," Lydia said and flashed a becoming smile at Slocum.

He touched two fingers to the brim of his black hat and walked toward the creek.

"Don't leave us here too long," Fenster said.

Slocum crossed the creek, stepping on stones, and reached the other side. He waved to the three people and walked down the road. Their tracks were plain to see. They had been running, at least part of the time.

There were many such roads in the mountains, but he was not familiar with this one. From the looks of it, it had not been used for some time, at least a year, he figured. Woodcutters would have had to climb up the mountainsides, cut down trees, trim them, and use mules or horses to skid them back to the road, where they loaded them on wagons. He was surprised that they hadn't built a ramp of some sort so that they could just roll the logs onto the wagons. They had done it the hard way.

The women and Fenster had not come far. After he rounded a bend in the road, he saw what was left of the wagon train. Beyond was the main road. He wondered why the wagon master had turned off on this scrawny little road.

Then, as he reached the wagons, he saw why. On the other side of the road someone had put up a sign that pointed up the logging road.

The sign was crude, painted on a board with one end coming to a point.

The sign read: BIG TIMBER, 2 MILES

Big Timber was at least ten miles away on that main road.

3

Slocum walked down to the road and put his shoulder to the pole holding up the sign. He pushed and the road sign tipped over. Then he walked onto the logging road and surveyed the tilted wagons, the coach, the scattered garments, the opened suitcases, the jewelry boxes.

Then he looked at the dead.

One man was slumped over the seat of the coach. There was an arrow buried in his chest. Another man lay on the ground nearby. He, too, had an arrow through his back. Slocum examined the fletching, the feathers, the markings on the shaft.

"Crow," he said to himself.

Two women in flowered cotton dresses lay in the bed of one of the wagons. Their throats were slit. A young man lay across the seat, his head split open, his brains leaking out like boiled oatmeal. The women's dresses were pulled up around their waists, their panties slit open, their legs spread. They had been violated, Slocum could see. Brutally violated.

He walked among the dead and tried to imagine how so many had died so quickly.

The bandits had slit open the boot of the stagecoach and some of the contents had tumbled out. These lay in a heap on the ground. However, inside the boot, strapped in, were two black guitar cases. They were difficult to see against the black crepe at the back of the boot. Someone had kicked through the stack of valises that had fallen to the ground, and had opened each one and left them all gaping like the mouths of large dark birds. A few tintypes lay scattered on the ground, fading yellowish likenesses of hardscrabble farmers, their wives and children standing before graying frame houses or paintless barns cobbled together from odd-sized boards of whipsawed lumber on some flat and lifeless prairie in Kansas or Nebraska.

He saw horse tracks in a maze around the wagons and coach, and signs that some of the riders had ventured up the road and into the woods, no doubt searching for those who had escaped. He saw tracks that might have been made by Jasmine, Lydia, and Fenster that had somehow been overlooked by the robbers.

He also found the place where the bushwhackers had waited for the small wagon train to turn up the old wood-cutters' road. In a copse of spruce trees atop a small ridge were signs that men on horseback had waited there. The soft ground was scarred with the hieroglyphs of shod and unshod horses, thin scraps of paper from partially smoked cigarettes, a few piles of human excrement, and holes where men had pissed onto the fallen pine needles. One patch of snow was filled with such holes that had a yellowish tinge from the urine.

He followed the tracks he thought might have belonged to the two women and the little man in the dark suit. It was plain to see how they had escaped notice. They had scrambled up a vein of limestone rock and into the shelter of spruce and fir trees, then continued on a course parallel to the road.

Evidently, none of the raiders had seen the women and

the little man make their escape, and the buried limestone, like the spine of a prehistoric beast, ran straight up a steep ridgeline that would have been difficult for a man on horseback to climb. The trees were thick and bushy. There was a splintered juniper where a bull elk had sharpened its antlers during the previous fall season. Its trunk was splayed as if it had been struck by a massive lightning bolt. Slocum had seen such trees before and had even seen elk attack a juniper during the rut.

As he was about to leave the ridge top, Slocum heard a sound that froze him in his tracks.

He moved his head slowly, less than an inch at a time, to focus on the direction from whence the sound had come. He heard it again, higher up the slope. He did not move for several seconds. He just listened.

At first he thought he might be hearing a chipmunk or a squirrel scurrying through the leaves. But after a moment, he knew that it was something else. Something big.

He eased his rifle up and let the barrel fall onto his left hand, which was opened like a cradle. His right hand slid down to the stock, just behind the lever. He gripped the forestock with his left hand and slowly eased down the lever. The breech opened and a cartridge slid from the magazine into the barrel. He slammed the lever back into place, sealing the breech, and dropped to his knees behind a pine tree.

There was a rustle of branches above him and the sound of someone breathing.

"Oh, damn it," he heard someone say.

The voice was unmistakably female. A woman's voice, without a doubt.

Slocum peered from behind the tree. He kept his head low and his rifle at the ready.

Something black moved like a shadow through the brush above him.

Then he heard something fly through the air. It wasn't a bird. He ducked instinctively, but when the object landed off to his left, he pulled his rifle away from the tree and whirled. Something struck the ground with a thud, then rolled downhill.

Slocum craned his neck to see what it was. Leaves and pine needles rose and fell as the object passed over them.

He thought he heard something behind him.

But before he could turn his head, something hard slammed into the base of his skull. He felt his body lose its balance and pitch forward.

Everything went black, and multicolored stars danced in Slocum's head. He tried to open his eyes, but the stars dimmed and tumbled into a Stygian pit of blackness.

All the world inside Slocum's head went dark.

Then there was an emptiness that was the void, where nothing existed.

He slipped into unconsciousness, where he hovered weightless over a churning sea that was all black and very deep.

4

Slocum dreamed that he was on a high cliff, a bleak lime-stone cliff that towered above a green sea. He could hear seagulls calling, their screeches like the voices of lost souls. Cottony clouds floated in a blue sky, and as he gazed up-ward, the earth began to spin beneath him. He felt himself topple from the cliff. His clothing flew off his body as he plummeted toward the water. He struck the sea face first and gasped for air as his mouth tasted water.

Slocum opened his eyes as he was jerked from the dream. He clawed for his pistol, and his fingers struck an empty holster. He reached for his rifle as he wiped water from his eyes.

That was when he saw the ugly snouts of a sawed-off double-barreled shotgun just inches from his face.

"What the hell . . ." Slocum gasped as he spat drops of water from his mouth.

"Mister, I got both barrels cocked and my finger's ready to pull the trigger. You got two seconds to tell me who you are and what you're doing here."

"I'm John Slocum," he said as he touched the sore spot

17

on the back of his head. "I'm here to see what happened with the folks in that wagon train. Have I used up my two seconds?"

He looked up at the woman who held the shotgun. She laughed and lowered the weapon. She was tall and slender, with a regal face that seemed to be chiseled to perfection. She was dressed in black and wore a simple strand of pearls around her alabaster neck.

He heard the whisper of the twin hammers as she eased them back down to the half-cock position.

"I took away your pistol and moved your rifle, just in case you were one of those jaspers who jumped the wagons. I didn't think you were, but I had to be sure."

"That was quite a whack you gave me."

"Like I said, I didn't know who you were. Where did you come from?"

"You were with the wagons?" Slocum said. "How did you get away?"

"I was in the stagecoach when it turned off the main road. I knew something was wrong. I saw horses' legs up on that ridge, in the trees, and I dove for the opposite door, opened it, and pushed out the other passengers. I whispered to them as I ran. Told them to follow me. I had the Greener with me and I hid out. The two other women and their companion just kept running. I don't know where they went, or even if they got away and are still alive."

"They are," Slocum said. "They told me what happened. I came down to have a look for myself."

He steadied himself against a tree and got to his feet. He was a little woozy, but he stood there, bracing himself against the pine until the dizziness went away.

"Your pistol and rifle are up there where I spent the night," she said. "Follow me."

The woman led him to a depression in the earth. He saw where she had lain. There were large chunks of pine bark and juniper limbs piled next to the small ditch.

He reached down and picked up his pistol, then hefted his rifle out of the sunken makeshift bed.

"You stayed there all night?"

"It's what I call a debris shelter. My husband taught me how to survive in the mountains if I ever got bucked off my horse. You find a ditch or low spot and cover yourself with forest debris. I tucked myself into a ball and shivered all night. It was cold. But the shelter worked."

"Was your husband . . ."

He looked down the slope at the jumble of wagons and the tilted coach.

"He wasn't there, no. I was coming home from his funeral in Billings. I'm a widow woman," she said. He detected a note of sadness in her voice, a wistful strain in her tone that bespoke of loneliness and loss.

"I'm sorry," he said.

He walked over to where he had been knocked cold and picked up his hat. He brushed it off and set it squarely on his head. He fiddled in his pocket for a cheroot.

"Ma'am, I didn't get your name."

"I didn't give it. But it's Velva Granville. I was married to Albert Granville. I knew this wasn't the road to Big Timber because that's where Bert and I lived."

"Are you connected with Granville Outfitters in Big Timber?"

She nodded. "You know of it?"

"I saw the sign. I hired on to hunt for Ray Mallory at the Big Timber Hotel."

"Albert and I hunted for Nelson Montague of the Grant Hotel. Bert was a hunting and fishing guide. That's our store on Main Street."

"Why were you lugging that Greener with you in the coach?" Slocum asked.

"There have been Crow attacks on that road of late," she said. "Not many, but I didn't want my scalp hanging in some buck's lodge."

"So, you were prepared for an attack on the wagons?"

"Not at all," she said. "But there was a kind of wake for Albert after the funeral," she said. "It was held at the Absaroka Hotel, and there was talk of white men organizing some of the Crow tribe to rob people from the Little Big Horn to the Yellowstone. It was just talk, but from what I saw yesterday, I believe the gossip to be true. There were white men with those Crow braves and they ran the whole show. They were looking for something, or someone."

"What makes you say that?" Slocum asked.

"The man I took to be the leader of the bunch kept yelling, 'Where is she?' and 'Where is that bitch?'"

Slocum felt his stomach swirl with moths and he got a sick feeling.

"He say a name?"

"No. He was just looking for some bitch. I didn't think it was a favorite female dog of his."

"One of the women down there who was defiled?" he asked.

"You mean raped, don't you? That's what they did to them before they cut their throats. I can still hear their awful screams."

"Yes, the women who were raped."

"I don't think so. The Crow braves violated the women first. Then, from what I heard, and what little I saw, some of the white men took their turns."

"Well, Velva, here's the situation," Slocum said. "I've got two horses up on the mountain and two pack mules. Ray's kid, Donnie, is up there waiting for me. You can either walk up the road to where Lydia, Jasmine, and Fenster are waiting for me in a cave, or you can hike up that mountain yonder with me and we'll all ride down and pick up the three people. We'll have to double up, but we can all ride back to Big Timber. As the crow flies."

"I'll go with you," she said, "although I wish had on

boots instead of these severe widow's shoes. And my dress is beginning to look like widow's weeds."

"You can ride a mule back down or you can ride with me, Mrs. Granville," he said. "Suit yourself."

"I'll look over the mules. Just so I don't ride with Donnie."

"You know the kid?"

"He hung around our store. Bert threw him out more than once. I don't think he has all his marbles, that kid. Or if he does, they're all chipped and lopsided."

Slocum laughed.

"Let's go," he said. "Donnie's probably worried that I've been gone so long."

"I'm surprised you left him with your horses and mules. That kid couldn't watch corn grow without peeing his pants. He'd be scared of the scarecrow."

"I think I know what you mean, Mrs. Granville."

"Please, Mr. Slocum. Call me Velva. I'm no longer Mrs. Granville. My husband is dead and I'm his widow. May I call you John?"

"Velva," he said with a grin, "you can call me anything you like."

She reached out and squeezed his arm in a friendly manner. The two walked down the slope at an angle, crossed the road, and began to climb the slope. Slocum knew exactly where Donnie was waiting with the horses and mules. Despite the shoes, Velva kept up with him. He chewed his cheroot down to a nub and finally spit it out.

The sun was straight above them in a blue and cloudless sky.

When the horses came into view, it was high noon in Montana, and Slocum was sweating like a horse himself.

5

Donnie was sound asleep inside the cave when Slocum and Velva approached. When he looked up, after Slocum kicked the sole of his boot, Donnie's eyes widened in fear. His jaw dropped and a tiny squeak issued from his throat.

"Get up, Donnie," Slocum said.

"Gawd," Donnie exclaimed, "I thought you two was the undertakers and I had plumb died."

Velva laughed. Slocum frowned.

"Well, you're both wearin' black," Donnie said as he scooted out of the cave on his butt. His single-shot rifle was lying next to him. He picked it up.

"That's not loaded, is it?" Slocum said as Donnie stood up.

"No sir, but I got a bullet in my pocket ready to load 'case a bear come up on me."

"You ride one of the mules, Donnie," Slocum said. "We're leavin' this place."

"Did you find my elk?"

Slocum stopped dead in his tracks as he walked toward his horse, a Morgan gelding he called Ferro, the Spanish word for iron.

"Your elk?" he said.

"Well, I shot it, didn't I?"

Donnie wore a look of genuine surprise on his face. Velva looked at him indulgently, as one would perceive an addled child.

"Technically, yes," Slocum said. "You shot it, but you only wounded it. The elk got away."

"You ain't much of a hunter, I'm thinkin'," Donnie said.

"Leave the panniers here," Slocum said to him. "You mount up on that jenny and lead the other mule. Velva, you can ride Donnie's horse."

The horses were still saddled. Slocum untied the reins from an alder bush and put one foot in the stirrup. He watched as Velva climbed into the saddle of Donnie's horse. He could see that she was no neophyte. She climbed into the saddle, tucked her skirt under her, and swung a bare left leg over the horn. Slocum couldn't take his eyes off that bare leg until he felt her gaze on him. He smiled and climbed into the saddle.

"We can talk about those two things later, John, if you like," she said, a look of abject innocence on her face.

"What two things?" he asked.

"That look on your face and my bare leg," she said, her voice a soft purr in his ear that was almost like a caress.

"Oh yeah," he said. "I couldn't help looking at it."

His look was now decidedly sheepish.

She reached behind the cantle and untied Donnie's bedroll. She wrapped the shotgun in the blanket and placed it back where it had been. She tied the thongs that held the bedroll in place.

"You didn't unload that Greener," Slocum observed.

"An unloaded gun is as useful as teats on a boar," she said.

"Let's hope it doesn't go off on its own accord," Slocum said.

"Does your gun go off on its own accord, John?"

He looked directly into her dark brown eyes and saw the mirthful expression on her face. She returned his stare with a bold look of her own. He felt something inside him squirm as if she had impaled a part of him on a metal skewer.

"Almost never," he said with a wry twist of his lips.

Velva made a small moue with her mouth.

"That's good to know," she said.

Slocum let it pass.

"Ready?" he said to her and Donnie.

"Lead the way," she said.

Slocum looked back and saw that Donnie was mounted on the jenny and had the reins of the jack in his hand. His rifle was laid across his lap, where he held it with his right hand. Slocum slid his rifle into its boot and started down the slope at an angle.

"What happened to my elk?" Donnie asked as they cleared the brush halfway down the slope.

"Who knows?" Slocum said. "It got away. Probably doomed to die a slow death."

"Darn," Donnie said, and Slocum vowed to teach him how to curse if they ever hunted together again.

Slocum zigzagged down to the road. Fenster and the two women watched as they crossed the road.

"Didn't think you was ever comin' back for us," Fenster said, clearly annoyed. "We're starving and thirsty as all get-out."

"We're all hungry," Slocum said. He swung out of the saddle and stepped up to his saddlebags. "I've got jerky and hardtack in here, and my canteen's full." He handed Fenster some dried beef strips wrapped in a towel and unslung his canteen from the saddle horn. He plucked another towel from the saddlebag and handed it to Jasmine. "Hardtack," he said. "And I do mean hard. Like a rock."

"I'm not that hungry," Jasmine said.

"I am," Lydia said, and snatched the folded towel from Slocum's hand.

"Hello, ladies," Velva said. "I was hoping you were both still alive. Mr. Fenster," she said with a nod to the little man.

"What about the others?" Jasmine asked.

Velva lowered her head.

"All dead," Slocum said.

"The two ladies, Mrs. Gilbert and Rosie Coombs?"

"I'm sorry," Slocum said.

Jasmine shuddered.

"We're going to ride over to Big Timber," Slocum said. "I'll see to it that you three find lodging at the Big Timber Hotel. I'll see the sheriff, get a wagon, and go with him to clean up the mess."

"Our guitars are there," Lydia said as she chewed on a strip of jerky. "Or they were."

"I think they're still there."

"We'll need those right away," Jasmine said.

Slocum looked at the two women. He read genuine concern in their faces.

"You going to sing for your supper in Big Timber?" he asked.

"That's what we do," Jasmine said, a defensive tone to her voice. "We have an offer to perform at the Big Timber Hotel."

Slocum looked at Donnie. He shrugged.

"I've been at the hotel for the past month and a half. Ray never mentioned it and I never saw anyone perform there."

"We have a letter," Lydia said. "An invitation. Don't we, Leroy?"

Fenster patted his suit coat. "Got it right here. It wasn't from nobody named Ray, though."

"Ray Mallory owns the hotel," Slocum said.

"It ain't signed by no Ray Mallory neither," Fenster said, a slight trace of belligerence in his tone.

"Let me see the letter," Slocum said.

"It ain't none of your business, Mr. Slocum," Fenster said. His tone was now decidedly belligerent.

"Oh, Leroy, let him see it," Jasmine said. She drank from the canteen, sipping from it as if she were testing it for a poisonous taste.

Fenster reached into his inside coat pocket and produced a letter. It was in a plain envelope, which he handed to Slocum. Slocum opened the envelope and withdrew the letter. It was on hotel stationery, all right, the same stationery that was in a drawer in his room at the hotel.

He looked at the signature.

The letter was handwritten in a broad scrawl. The signature was large over a printed name.

"This is signed by someone named Leonard Baskin," he said. "Donnie, anyone named Baskin at your pa's hotel??

"Nope," Donnie said. He slid from the jenny's back and walked over to Slocum. He looked at the letter.

"Recognize the name or the handwriting, Donnie?" Slocum asked.

"Nope. That's the stationery we put in the rooms. My pa has his own stationery with his name big on the top. And after his name, it says 'proprietor.' That's on all his stationery. Someone's pullin' your leg, lady, you'll pardon the expression."

"Why, that's outrageous," Jasmine said.

"Someone wanted you to be in Big Timber real bad," Slocum said. "Because this letter is not genuine."

Jasmine's face flushed a pale crimson. She was plainly humiliated. Lydia looked as if someone had delivered a straight punch to her solar plexus. Her complexion turned to paste and she looked sick.

"After Lydia's father died," Jasmine said, "I made a big mistake. I married a man who was kind to me. He was a wolf in sheep's clothing. He wanted to take over my life. He became very brutal, and his demands on me were disgusting and savage. He beat me and he chased after Lydia. I divorced this man and he went into a rage. He said that I would pay for rejecting him."

"Who is this man?" Slocum asked.

"I hesitate to even speak his name," she said. Tears welled up in her eyes and she choked back a sob.

"His name is Bruno Valenti," Lydia said.

Velva gasped when she heard the name. They all looked at her as if they were one person.

"Bruno? Is that your former husband's given name?" Velva asked.

Jasmine nodded. "He—he lives in Saint Louis. Or did, when I divorced him."

"Why?" Slocum asked. "Why do you ask? Do you know the man?"

Velva drew herself up to full height. She was a tall woman and towered over Fenster, Lydia, and Jasmine. She looked as regal as any queen, and her dark eyes flashed with streaks of sunlight that looked like lightning bolts.

"That was a name I heard some of the bandits use," she said. "They yelled out 'Bruno,' and Bruno was the man who kept saying, 'Where is the bitch?' and 'The bitch ain't here.' Curly black hair, a scarred face, a big barrel of a chest, hairy arms."

Jasmine broke down. She buried her face in her hands and sobbed into them.

"That's Bruno," Lydia said. "I can't believe it. You described him perfectly. He's a very vicious man and I thought we were rid of him."

Velva walked over and put an arm around Jasmine.

"There, there," she said. "We'll look after you, Jasmine. Won't we, John?"

Slocum nodded. His jaw turned to iron as he thought about the savagery of the attack on the coach and wagons, the needless slaughter of innocent people.

He knew, deep down, that they probably had not heard the last of Bruno Valenti. For he was a man bent on revenge. He would surely come after Jasmine and try to kill her. Slocum had met such scoundrels before. They could not stand the thought of a woman they wanted being with another man. If they couldn't have her, they pledged that no one could have her.

He felt sorry for Jasmine, and for Lydia.

They would bear watching as long as they were in Big Timber, until Bruno Valenti was in jail or dead.

6

Slocum led the party in his charge over the ridge tops in a more or less straight line, avoiding the road. Velva rode double with him. Jasmine and Lydia rode Donnie's horse, while Donnie rode the jenny, and Fenster rode the bone-jarring jack. They descended the last hill down to the Boulder River and crossed just below Spring Creek. The waters were swift but shallow since the river was over its banks with spring runoff.

They entered Big Timber, a small, quiet town bordered on two sides by the Boulder and the Yellowstone Rivers. Slocum pulled in at the Big Timber Hotel on Main Street, a block from the Grant Hotel, which they had passed moments before.

Slocum dismounted and, in gentlemanly fashion, helped Jasmine and Lydia dismount. They tied the horses and mules to the hitchrail.

"I'll get you settled, then see the sheriff," Slocum told Jasmine.

"I'll go with you, John," Velva said. Slocum was surprised, but did not show his surprise to Velva. He just nodded. He ushered Jasmine, Lydia, and Fenster to the desk. Donnie followed them, scratching at an itch on his butt.

The clerk looked up.

"Oh, hello, Mr. Slocum," he said. Then he looked at the others. "What do we have here? More guests."

"Check them in. I'll talk to Mr. Mallory when I finish with the sheriff."

"And who will pay the bill?" asked the clerk, whose name was Alfred Duggins.

"Don't worry it about it, Alfred. These people were attacked by bandits and Crow Indians. I'm taking Sheriff Jenner to see where it happened."

"I see," Duggins said.

Velva gave Slocum a look, rolling her eyes at the situation.

He knew what she meant. Clerks and shopkeepers had their own codes, their special set of rules for dealing with the public, and any variation in their mindless routine put them off-balance and led to confusion.

"Just sign the register," Duggins said. He turned the open ledger around and shoved it forward. "Three rooms?"

"Just two," Jasmine said. "My daughter and I will share one, and Mr. Fenster will have one to himself."

"I see," Duggins said. He was beginning to make sense of the situation. He was now on firmer ground, Slocum surmised, and he shot a look at Velva, who nodded, almost imperceptibly. Donnie stood next to a potted plant and mopped his face with a handkerchief.

"No luggage?" Duggins said. He craned his neck to peer over the counter.

"Alfred," Slocum said, "they were on the Bozeman stage. It was wrecked and they barely escaped with their lives. We'll salvage what we can and haul their belongings back here to the hotel."

"I see," Duggins said, and Slocum knew he didn't see a damned thing. No luggage was a sign to Duggins that the guests were without visible means of support and might skip their bill in the dead of night.

He looked up then and acknowledged Velva.

"Oh, hello, Mrs. Granville. So sorry about your loss."

"I was in that stagecoach, Alfred," she said. "We've all been through a lot. I was returning from my husband's funeral in Billings when we were attacked."

"Oh, yes, of course," Duggins spluttered. "I should have known."

He looked down at the register as Fenster signed his name, turned it around, and pushed it toward the clerk. Duggins read the names.

"You're the Lorraines," he said to Jasmine.

"We are," Jasmine said.

"Why, I saw you and your daughter perform in San Francisco last year. You were sensational. Such beautiful voices."

"Why, thank you, Alfred," Jasmine said. "Maybe you'll hear us somewhere in Big Timber."

"Oh, that would be just wonderful. We have a small ballroom here in the hotel, with a little stage and . . . well, that would just be peachy."

"Will someone show us to our rooms?" Fenster asked. His impatience was evident in the nervous tap of his fingers on the counter.

"I'll get your keys and show you to your rooms. They're all on the second floor. Just take those stairs over there." He pointed to a wide stairway that led up to a balcony. "I'll be right with you."

Velva gave Jasmine a hug and then turned to Lydia, but she was already walking toward the stairs with Fenster.

"Let's go see the sheriff," Slocum said to Velva.

"Can I go with you?" Donnie said. "Maybe I could help."

Slocum hesitated, but he saw Velva give her approval with a slight nod of her head.

"Yeah, Donnie, you can go with us. Sheriff might want you to drive back one of the wagons."

"Thanks, Mr. Slocum. I ain't got nothin' to do here in town anyways."

"No, Donnie," Velva said, her voice a silky purr, "there's not much to do in Big Timber."

The three of them walked the half block to the sheriff's office. They passed a few people looking into store windows, a pair of women chatting together, and an old man with a cane who was headed toward the corner saloon, The Gray Cat.

"So, you know Dave Jenner?" Velva said.

"I met him when I first came to town," Slocum said.

"When did you first come to town?"

"About three days ago. I was up in Billings on business and saw a flyer seeking the services of a meat hunter. Donnie's father."

"That explains a lot," Velva said.

"What do you mean?"

"Ray Mallory and my husband got in a big fight a month or so ago. We provided game to Ray and to the Grant Hotel, but Ray thought we charged too much. And my husband refused to take Donnie with us when we went after elk and mule deer."

Donnie's eyebrows rose, but he said nothing.

"Maybe I can smooth that over for you, Velva," Slocum said. "I don't plan to work for Ray beyond the fall."

"His hotel is going to need wild game. It's one of the specialties of Big Timber. We have visitors from all over the world. Many of them expect to eat wild turkey, pheasant, antelope, elk, and deer when they stay in the hotels."

"Maybe we can join forces while I'm here," Slocum said.

Velva smiled.

"I'd like that," she said.

The sheriff's office was a small log building near the

end of Main Street, which was only about five blocks long. A lone horse, a mottled gray, stood hipshot, its reins wrapped around the hitchrail. Its mane and tail were clipped short. The three walked through the leather-hinged door into the sheriff's office.

Sheriff David Jenner was leaning back in his chair, his long legs stretched out, his booted feet propped up on the desk. He was going through a stack of wanted flyers, a small corncob pipe jutting from one side of his mustache-framed mouth.

"Hello, Dave," Velva said in that silky smooth voice of hers.

Jenner looked up. His pale blue eyes, eyes that were almost gray, scanned the faces of Slocum, Velva, and Donnie.

"I see you're back from the funeral in Billings, Velva," he said, retracting his legs like a crane ready to lift its wings in flight. "Slocum. Thought you and Donnie there were off hunting elk."

"You don't miss much, do you, Sheriff?" Slocum said.

"Hell, it's a small town. Ain't easy to miss what goes on." Jenner stood up.

"What brings you folks to my humble office?" he said.

Slocum told him. Velva filled in the actual details of the ambush, including the names of the people who were killed.

Jenner pursed his lips and let out a low whistle. "Shit fire," he said. "I'd better haul ass down there and get them folks back here for a decent burial. You say them Injuns and white renegades stole all the horses?"

"That's right," Velva said.

"Well, we're gonna need to take some extra horses to haul them wagons and that stage into town. Damn, you say Will Purdy was kilt? He's been drivin' that Billings to Bozeman stage for nigh onto six years, I reckon."

"There were only four of us who managed to escape," Velva said. "A mother and her daughter and their manager. They're staying at the Big Timber."

"Well, first things first. I'll talk to them folks later. Meanwhile, I got to get a posse together and some extry horses to take down there where you say all this happened."

"We'll go with you," Slocum said.

"You and Donnie, you mean?"

"And me," Velva said. "And, you know, Albert and I have a stable. You can use my horses. I want to change out of these widow's weeds anyway."

"Well, shit fire," Jenner said. "Let's get a-goin' then. That makes my job a whole hell of a lot easier."

He grabbed his hat off a wooden hat rack and took a Winchester and a box of cartridges from a drawer at the bottom of the cabinet.

Jenner stuck his rifle in its boot, put the box of cartridges in his saddlebag, and mounted the mottled bobtailed gray.

"Our horses are at the Big Timber," Slocum said.

"I'll ride old Mousey here so's we can leave from there."

"You don't lock your office?" Slocum asked.

"Nobody's in the jail and ain't nobody wants in that I know of. We got a pretty quiet town here. At least until now."

They walked back to the hotel and mounted up.

"We passed close to my house when we rode into town, when we crossed Spring Creek," Velva told Slocum. "I'll show you the stable. You can take what horses we'll need while I change clothes."

"I didn't see your house," Slocum said.

"You will," she said, and it seemed to Slocum that she meant more than her words indicated, as if there was a promise in her statement.

He tried to remember where they had crossed the Boulder and if he had seen any signs of habitation nearby. But the country here was still new and strange to him, and he had seen no sign of a house in that rugged place above Big Timber.

They rode up Main Street toward Spring Creek, and

passed the last homely little frame house made of crude, whipsawed lumber and then they were on rocky terrain. The road paralleled the Boulder River, but Slocum didn't know how far it went. He figured it probably stretched way up in the timber, the big timber from whence the town drew its name.

"Did you know the two women who were killed?" Slocum asked Jenner as they rode toward Spring Creek.

"Rosie Coombs was a widder woman who made fried pies for the hotels here," Jenner said. "She went to Billings to buy apples and flour. She did that once a month. Camille Gilbert never did marry. She had a young man she was supposed to marry, but he went off to war and was killed at Manassas Junction."

"That's where my father was killed," Slocum said. "Seems a long time ago. He was from Georgia, like me."

"Camille Gilbert was my auntie," Jenner said. "She lived with me. I got a two-story place down near the Yellowstone. Auntie Camille lived in an upstairs room. I'm goin' to miss her."

"You might not recognize her, Dave."

"Oh, I'll recognize her all right. I might not be able to see her real good, though."

"Why is that?"

"I 'spect I'll be cryin' pretty hard. I loved that dear woman. My mother's sister, God rest their souls."

"I'm sorry I was the bearer of such bad news, Dave," Slocum said.

"I'd like to get my hands on the bastards who raped them women and killed them. But there's just me wearin' a badge in this town, and most of the able-bodied men are dumb as a sack full of sash weights."

"I'd like to catch them, too, Sheriff," Slocum said. "If you need an extra hand . . ."

"What I need is an extra hand and an extra gun," Jenner said.

He looked over at Slocum. Looked him up and down.

"Looks like you'd do just fine," he said. "I could use some help."

"You got it," Slocum said.

They rounded a bend in the road then turned off to the right on what appeared to be a tree-lined lane. The trees were aspen with bright white trunks that were scarred by dark patches. In the distance, Slocum saw the outline of a large home, surrounded by a grassy sward.

His horse neighed and bobbed its head up and down.

"Ferro smells your horses, I reckon," he said to Velva.

"You and Ferro are both welcome," she said, and her voice melted something inside him. He felt a tug at his heart and, when he looked at her regal face, a tug somewhere else, somewhere deep in his loins.

7

Velva led the party to the rear of the large, three-story house that sprawled over a quarter acre of land. Slocum was surprised at the size of the livery stable, and the enclosed corral where horses drank at water troughs and ate from grain bins. There were twenty-four stalls inside the large stable.

"The tall sorrel gelding with four white stockings and a star blaze is my horse," Velva said. "My saddle's the first one you see in the tack room. I won't be long."

"I'll saddle your horse for you," Slocum said.

"That would be very nice of you," she said as she swung out of the saddle, as graceful as any woman Slocum had ever seen. When she rode, she seemed part of the horse. The tall gelding that was hers was a beautiful animal, a russet horse that stood at least sixteen hands high.

"Let's get bridles and ropes, Donnie," Jenner said. "How many horses do we need, Slocum?"

"Four for the stage and there are two wagons that'll need a horse each."

"All right, six horses," Jenner said. He and Donnie followed Slocum to the tack room. Slocum picked up Velva's

39

saddle and blanket from a sawhorse. A bridle hung from the saddle horn. Like the saddle, it had silver fittings. Jenner started handing Donnie bridles that were hanging on wooden pegs on the back wall of the tack room. He found a coiled manila rope that was fifty feet long and grabbed that.

By the time Slocum had saddled the roan gelding and bridled six horses, Velva emerged from the back door of the house. She was wearing tight-fitting riding pants and a dark blue blouse that fit just as tight. She wore a flat-crowned Spanish hat with leather thongs that looped down beneath her chin. The band around the crown had a geometric design in red, blue, and yellow. She walked to Donnie's horse and pulled his bedroll off the saddle, removing her sawed-off shotgun. She carried a small black bag slung over her shoulders. It rattled when she walked.

"Extra shot shells," she said as she tied the shotgun behind the cantle of her saddle.

"I didn't say anything," Slocum said.

"No, but you were looking and listening to the rattle of brass in my bag."

"You're hard to miss," he said.

She stood close to him and he smelled the scent of fresh perfume she had dabbed behind her ears and on her wrists. His nose crinkled.

"I see you have a sense of smell, too, John," she said, her voice as mellifluous as a harp's delicate arpeggios.

"You smell pretty good, lady," he said.

Her face took on a glow at the compliment.

"We ready?" Jenner said. "The horses are hooked up. Donnie, you think you can hold on to that rope until we get to the massacre site?"

"Yeah, I think so."

They set out, back down the road, down Main Street to the Bozeman–Billings Road. Sheep grazed along the Yellowstone and the lady rancher waved to them as they passed, east of town. On the way to the ambush site, antelope gamboled on the prairie and the blue sky seemed to stretch forever. Few words were spoken.

"There's the sign they put up," Slocum said to Jenner. "I knocked it down."

"And I see the wagons and the stagecoach," the sheriff said. "Godamighty, Will should have knowed better."

"Maybe there was somebody standing by that sign with a rifle who waved him up that logging road," Slocum said.

"Well, I'm damned sure goin' to check it out. Tracks tell a tale, you know."

Slocum nodded.

He helped Donnie put the bodies of Rosie and Camille into one of the wagons and covered them with a blanket. Then they hitched the horses to the wagons while Jenner and Velva looked at the two dead women. Jenner picked up two fifty-pound flour sacks and stacked them close to the tailgate. Tears flooded his face as he looked at his dead and violated aunt and her friend. Slocum and Jenner put the bodies of Will Purdy and his shotgunner in the coach.

"Jed Loomis was ridin' shotgun," Jenner said. "He wasn't more than twenty or twenty-one. His ma and pa will take it hard."

"These men were slaughtered. Shotgun was still under the top seat," Slocum said.

Jenner and Slocum loaded the bodies of several other men into the stagecoach with Will Purdy and Jed Loomis, then hitched four horses to the stage. Slocum closed the boot and turned the rig around, drove it onto the main road.

"Velva, can you drive this coach back to Big Timber?" Jenner asked.

"Yes, but why?"

"Me and Slocum are going to study these tracks, see if we can figure out where them Injuns and white renegades come from, how long they waited here, and so on."

"Where do you want it?" she asked.

"Park it in front of the Big Timber. Slocum and I'll meet you there in the bar."

"I might be in the dining room by then," she said.

"Don't let nobody touch nothin' till I get back," Jenner said.

"All right," she said. She dismounted and tied her horse up to the back of the coach and climbed into the seat. She released the brake and smiled at Slocum. He smiled back and waved a hand at her.

She snapped the reins and four horses pulled out.

"Donnie, you drive one of the wagons back, right behind Mrs. Granvillle. We'll bring the wagon with the women in it."

"Yes, sir," Donnie said. He tied his horse to the back of the wagon and climbed into the seat. That wagon was filled with lumber, nail kegs, and shingles. It belonged to the lumberyard, but nothing was written on the side panel. There was just a painted outline of a house on both side panels. But everyone in town knew that belonged to the Big Lion Lumber Company, a mile or so upriver on the Yellowstone.

"John, let's see what these tracks tell us," Jenner said as he climbed down from the wagon with the dead ladies lying blanketed in the bed.

The two men walked over to the knocked-down sign and studied the ground around it.

"Yep, just as I figured," Jenner said. "Two men stood their horses here. When they saw the stage comin', they probably told Purdy the road was out and he'd have to detour up that woodcutters' road."

"Would Purdy have known it was a trap?" Slocum asked.

"I don't know. Yet. Let's see where the bushwhackers waited for the stage and those wagons."

They walked up the road and sorted out all the tracks of the horses ridden by the bushwhackers. They traced their paths up a slight ridge and into the timber. In a small clearing, they saw where the Indians and white renegades had waited.

"But where did they come from?" Jenner asked.

Slocum walked out of the clearing and saw tracks leading down from the heavy timber.

"They came down this way," Slocum told Jenner. "And they rode back the same way. What's up there? Donnie and I were hunting just north of where those tracks might lead."

Jenner looked up through the pines and spruce, the fir trees and junipers.

"Loggers had cabins up thataway, if I remember right. "But they were built by prospectors long before they started cuttin' down timber."

"How many cabins?" Slocum asked.

"I don't know. Five or six maybe. I ain't been up there in four or five years. Lumberjacks had a big fight one night and had a little shootout. One of the loggers was killed and I had to investigate. Put a damper on the loggers, though. I don't think they ever came back to this part of the country. Now that I think of it, I think they moved up to the timber above Paradise Valley, near Livingston. It was pretty ugly."

"You might want to go up there again, see if there aren't Crow and white men living in those cabins."

"If you'll go with me, I'm game. Wouldn't want to go up there by myself."

"Just say the word," Slocum said.

The two men walked back down and tied their horses to the last wagon.

"You don't have to go up there with me, Slocum," Jenner said. "I mean I can't pay you nothin'. I might could deputize you."

"I'm a curious man, Dave," Slocum said. "I don't much like a mystery."

"You ought to think about becomin' a lawman."

The two climbed up into the seat of the buckboard. Slocum untied the reins and loosened the brake.

"I couldn't stay in one place long enough to watch over a town," Slocum said. "I got itchy feet."

Jenner laughed.

Slocum rattled the reins and yelled at the horse. It stepped out, bobbing and shaking its head and mane with a soft whicker.

On the way back, Slocum told Jenner about Jasmine's ex-husband, Bruno Valenti.

"Velva heard some of the raiders use his name."

"Was he out to kill his ex-wife?"

"Man couldn't have her. Maybe he didn't want anyone else to have her."

"Yeah," Jenner said. "That makes sense."

"It also means that Jasmine and maybe her daughter, Lydia, might still be in danger. A man like that won't give up too easy."

"He sounds like he could be a bad one."

"You ever heard of him before?" Slocum asked.

Jenner shook his head.

"I'll check through the dodgers in my office, but off-hand, his name don't ring a bell."

"I'm wondering how he got together a gang and enlisted the help of Crow to pull off this massacre."

"I have heard of some Crow off the reservation down in Wyoming. Mostly, they've been rustlin' sheep and cattle. Not around here, but over toward Billings and along the border."

"Well, I counted ten horses in that bunch that jumped the wagons," Slocum said.

"I counted eleven."

"Did you separate shod from unshod?" Slocum asked.

"No, I reckon I didn't."

"Well, six of those horses were unshod. That means Valenti has four or five men. You might need a posse to go after them if they're holed up in those loggers' cabins."

"I doubt if I could raise a posse in Big Timber. Livingston, maybe. Have to pay 'em, though, and there ain't nothin' in the kitty."

"Then you and I will have to scout that little settlement and be real careful we don't stir up a hornet's nest."

"Well, the cabins are on a wide ridge but there's timber all around them. Some bluffs, too, I think. We'd have to be real careful getting' up there without them knowin' we were there."

"They'll probably have Crow keepin' a lookout," Slocum said. "Keen eyes and keen ears."

"Yeah."

They spoke little the rest of the way to Big Timber. The blue sky was dotted with small cloud puffs out over the prairie, but behind the Absarokas, large thunderheads billowed up over the peaks. To the northwest, the Crazies were lit by sunshine angling off the Yellowstone, and they stretched over the land like a giant dinosaur, bristling with trees and rocks.

"We'll tie up at the Big Timber," Jenner said as they rolled onto Main Street. "I got a lot to do."

"I'm staying there. Holler if you need me," Slocum said.

"I imagine you might not spend tonight there, John."

"Why do you say that, Dave?"

"I saw the way Mrs. Granville was lookin' at you. When you wasn't lookin'."

"She's a handsome woman," Slocum said, "but she's a fresh widow. She's probably still grieving for her husband."

"Albert? Not a chance. There was no love lost between them two."

"They lived together."

"Separate bedrooms. Albert had him a gal in town and spent most of his time with her."

"I didn't know," Slocum said.

"Small towns, John," Jenner said. "They're full of secrets."

Slocum drew in a breath and let it out slow. He pulled up

to the hotel, set the brake, and thought about Velva Granville. There was more to that woman than met the eye, he decided.

But he would play it by ear. He wasn't a chaser. Women came to him. He never went after them. He wondered if Velva was a hunter of wild game. He wondered if she was a huntress of men, as well.

He climbed down from the wagon and untied Ferro, wrapped his reins around the hitchrail.

He glanced in the stagecoach and saw that it was empty. Then he looked in the bed of the wagon. The two dead women were gone.

At least, he thought, Big Timber must have an undertaker.

And perhaps many secrets.

8

The lobby was crowded with townspeople when Slocum and Jenner entered the hotel. The crowd buzzed with questions and some of the women were crying, dabbing their eyes with handkerchiefs. An old man rushed up to Jenner and began to spray him with rapid-fire questions. Donnie was surrounded by a small group of men and women who wanted to know all the gory details of the ambush.

Jasmine and Lydia sat on a sofa, tuning up their guitars. Leroy Fenster was telling people about the Lorraines. Ray Mallory stood in front of the counter, watching with interest. Behind him, at the check-in desk, the clerk stared at the assemblage with wide eyes.

Some of the townspeople, when they saw Sheriff Jenner, left their groups and surrounded him. They hurled questions at him so fast that he held up his hands in surrender.

He looked at Slocum with the appeal of a drowning man in his eyes. Slocum smiled and walked toward the entrance to the saloon and dining room. He slipped through the people almost without notice and then saw Velva beckoning to him from the foyer that led to the other sections of the hotel.

"It's a madhouse in there," she said. "You're lucky you escaped."

"Jenner's getting all the questions," he said.

"Trouble is, he probably doesn't have any answers."

Slocum laughed.

Velva led him to a door midway down the hall to the dining room. These were actually batwing doors that swung both ways. They entered a saloon that was dimly lit with lamps inset into plastered walls and by a candelabra that hung high in the center of the room. She led him to a table for two in a dark corner and beckoned to a barmaid who stood at the end of the bar, talking to the bartender.

"What do you drink?" she asked.

"Kentucky bourbon," Slocum said. "Straight and at least a week old."

Velva smiled.

"I like your sense of humor, John."

"I think what I said was more wry than humorous, but thanks."

She looked up when the barmaid approached. She was an older woman, with gray hair tucked up in a bun. She looked like a former glitter gal with too much rouge on her cheeks, too much lipstick, and too much mascara on her eyelashes. She was chewing something that might have been chicle or tobacco. Her teeth were yellowed from smoking and she reeked of cheap perfume.

"Something for the gent?" she said. Her eyes fixed on Slocum as if she were recalling a youth that had long since fled.

"Kentucky bourbon, for the gentleman," Velva said. "Four fingers, neat."

"I'll see if we have any. My name's Gilda."

"Of course it is," Velva said, a trace of sarcasm in her voice.

"You want a refill?" she said to Velva. "Old Taylor, wasn't it?"

"Yes, it was, but no, I'm fine."

"That'll be four bits," Gilda said.

"When you bring the gentleman his drink, I'll give you fifty cents, Gilda."

Gilda let out a huff of a breath and whirled to prance back to the bar, her hefty hips asway as if she were already two sheets to the wind.

Slocum noticed a door on the back wall. As he looked at it, two men came through it and sidled up to the bar.

"Where does that door lead?" he asked Velva.

"That's the outside entrance," she said. "For those who don't want to come through the hotel lobby. There's a passageway between the hotel and the newspaper office next door. Those are two of the pressmen that just came in. They probably got out an extra about the murders and need some fortification."

"What's the name of the paper? I'd like to see their headlines on the ambush."

"The *Big Timber Gazette*. You can bet the headline and story will be lurid."

"It's all hearsay at this point. Not much of a story."

"I saw a reporter speaking to the Lorraines and their manager. I'll bet he got an earful." ·

"You talk to him?"

"Heavens, no. I don't want my name in the paper. Not in that one anyway."

Gilda brought Slocum his drink. He held the glass up and stared at the amber liquid when he moved it so that lamplight beamed through it.

"Thank you, Gilda," he said.

"Four bits, ma'am," Gilda said.

Velva dropped a fifty-cent piece on the table. Gilda snatched it up and hurried back to the bar.

"What are you looking for?" she asked Slocum.

"If this whiskey is rotgut," he said, "there will be little bits of stuff floating in it."

"Oh. Anything there?"

He set the glass down in front of him.

"Looks like pure Kentucky bourbon to me."

"You're a connoisseur," she said.

"In some quarters maybe."

"Women?" she said.

"That would be one of the quarters," he said with a smile. He held the glass up in front of her. "Here's to you, Velva. My first drink in Big Timber. Thanks."

She raised her glass and clinked it against his.

The two sipped from their glasses.

"I have Kentucky bourbon at my house," she said. "You can read the labels on the bottles. Some of them have not been opened."

"You have good taste," he said.

"In some quarters," she replied, her mouth curving in a seductive smile.

"Men?"

"That would be one of the quarters, John."

They both laughed together.

They drank and gazed at each other, talked about their lives in general, noncommittal terms. John did not ask any questions about Velva's late husband, and she didn't question him about his past life, beyond discovering that he was from Georgia and that he had fought for the South during the War.

From the lobby, they heard the plaintive strains of two guitars, then the close harmony of Jasmine and Lydia singing an old-time hymn.

"They're really good, aren't they?" Velva said.

"Yes. Their voices are pure and their harmony is excellent."

"Are you going back in there to listen?" she said as she drank the last of her drink.

"Still too many people for me."

"We can leave by that side door and go to my house,"

she said. "I can fix you a meal. You can drink some good bourbon."

"I accept your invitation," he said. He downed the last of his drink and she marveled that it had no effect on him. His eyes did not water, nor did he gasp for breath.

"Our horses are out front, but we'll leave through that side door. We'll scarcely be noticed." She glanced at the door.

He got up and took her hand, helped her out of her chair. She smiled and walked to the side door in regal fashion. John's stovepipe boots rang on the hardwood floor. They were outside before Gilda even noticed that they had left.

They rode to Velva's house near Spring Creek.

"Just tie your horse to the hitchrail. I have a stable boy who'll take care of our horses."

"I didn't see him when we were here before," Slocum said.

"He was in Livingston. But I see that he's back. He'll know what to do."

John looked around, but saw no one. They walked up the steps and she opened the door. A woman greeted them. She took Slocum's hat and bowed slightly to Velva.

"This is Clarissa Holmes, my maid and companion," Velva said. "Clarissa, this is Mr. Slocum. He'll be dining with me this evening."

"Yes'm, Miss Velva. I have a roast prepared, but—"

"That will be fine, Clarissa," she said with a look at Slocum, who nodded his agreement.

"Pleased to meet you, Mr. Slocum. She half curtsied and touched a hand to her bonnet, which held up dangling locks of silver-gray hair. She wore a small apron over her flowered print dress with its high round collar. Clarissa hung his hat on a coat tree and evaporated into the bowels of the house. Velva led him into a front room that was finely furnished with gleaming wood tables and comfortable Louis XIV chairs, bookcases, a globe, some Currier & Ives woodcuts in mahogany frames on the wall, a fireplace with a finely wrought flintlock from Lancaster County, Pennsylvania, its stock of curly maple polished to a high sheen. It was a man's room, but there were signs of a strong woman's touch, too, with paintings by Degas, Renoir, and Monet hanging in between the bookshelves. There was a large divan and two stuffed easy chairs, and in the center of the floor, a magnificent bear rug that was at least seven or eight feet in length.

"Grizzly," Velva said when Slocum looked at the rug in admiration. "I shot it, up in the Crazies."

"I'm impressed," he said.

She walked to a liquor cabinet and small bar. She opened it and took out a bottle of Kentucky bourbon that had not been opened. She held it up so that John could read the label.

"That's fine," he said.

"One of my favorites. Albert didn't drink much, but he liked his sherry. Have a seat, John. If you take the divan, we can be closer."

He sat on the divan and she poured two drinks in cut crystal tumblers. She bought them over, set them on the small table in front of the divan, and sat next to him.

"There," she said. "You seem to fit this room."

"It's a man's room mostly," he said as he looked around.

"Albert didn't care for it. He seldom came here. He sat on the back porch or on a stump out in the yard."

"So, the furnishings are all . . . you," he said.

"Yes. I've been to Paris and London. To Italy. Many of the books are ones I bought on the continent."

"You are full of surprises, Velva."

She lifted both glasses and handed him one. She touched her glass to his.

"Welcome to my lair," she said, and her voice was husky as if her words were stroked by a hand wearing a velvet glove.

"You sound like a vixen," he said as their glasses clinked together. "Your lair."

She laughed, and the sound was chromatic and soft, pleasing to his ear.

"Maybe I am a vixen," she said. "Maybe I lured you to my lair in order to devour you."

He looked at the bear rug.

"That's a nice soft rug," he said.

"Upstairs I have a large soft bed."

"A woman with two lairs?"

She laughed.

"One for seduction," she said. "The other for pleasure."

"Maybe I should be seducing you, Velva."

"Or we could seduce each other. If you're not terribly hungry, we could explore each other's passions and dine at dusk when the sky is soft and painted with pastels and we can have candlelight and wine."

"That's very seductive," he said, feeling that he and Velva were playing a kind of game, testing each other's desire with words instead of with groping hands.

"I would like to see more of your home," he said. "If you want me to."

"Will you spend the night?"

"It depends," he said.

"On what?"

"On where I'll sleep."

"If you sleep, John."

He laughed at her finely tuned sense of humor.

"I'm not as tired as I probably look," he said.

She reached out and traced a fingernail down the side of his cheek then along his jawline on the left side. It was a very sensual touch and he felt a tingle race up his spine as if a hairy-legged spider had crawled its length.

"You don't look tired at all," she said. "We can take our drinks upstairs if you like. I have another bar in my bedroom."

"If you think we'd be more comfortable . . ."

"Oh, it's a large, spacious room, a combination sitting

room and boudoir, such as I saw in Paris. I could live up there. There are bookshelves and paintings by Pissaro and Sisley, Manet, and Cezanne."

"I accept your kind invitation," he said. He stood up, with his drink in his hand. She picked hers up and took his arm.

"Follow me," she said, her voice almost a whisper.

"Lead the way," he said, and they strolled into the foyer, arm in arm, and ascended the stairs. She held on to him and the curving banister, their footfalls soft on the carpeted steps.

At the end of a long hall, she opened a door and led him inside a spacious bedroom. There was a large, canopied four-poster against the wall, with a fluffy comforter draped over it and silk-encased pillows. The room was faintly perfumed with scented furniture polish and rose petals floating in a large goblet half-filled with water. As Slocum looked around, he saw a bar and a liquor cabinet, and off to the side, there was a small sitting room with bookshelves and framed paintings bought in Paris and London. The rug under his feet was finely woven with intricate detail, and might have come from Persia.

"Welcome to my other lair," she said, standing on tiptoe to breathe into his ear.

Slocum felt his knees turn to a gelatinous mass and give way. She took his drink and set it with hers atop the bar. Then she walked back, closed the bedroom door, and turned a key in the lock.

She looked down at him, below his belt buckle.

"My," she said, "we've got to get you out of those trousers before you bust all your buttons."

In seconds, he was unbuckling his gun belt, and Velva was sitting on a chair, removing her boots.

The house was silent but for their breathing, and the bedroom seemed like something transplanted from a foreign land where all sorts of delights awaited the eager visitor.

9

Slocum gazed at Velva with a sense of wonder. She stood by the bed, divested of all her clothing, a study in feminine beauty. The delicate lines of her body seemed to draw light and shadow to her contours as if she were a model posing for a portrait in some artist's studio. She was beautiful, but she was also mysterious, the way she posed for him, with one leg close to the other, angled so as to partially preserve her modesty, while exposing the curve of her hips, the flat plane of her tummy, the slim ankles, and perky breasts, the breasts of a young woman in her prime.

"Are you just going to stare at me, John?" she asked in that purring tone of hers that was at once kittenish and, at the same time, alluring.

"You're a beautiful woman, Velva. Pleasing to the eye."

He walked toward her, his rigid staff swaying like a magical wand that drew her gaze to his loins.

"And," she said, husky-voiced with desire, "you are like a dark-haired Apollo, a Greek statue come to life."

He felt desire surge through his loins. He took her in his arms. They kissed with their lips, and then he found places on her neck and behind her ears where his lips touched her so that she quivered all over and arched her back.

They fell upon the bed in slow motion, their bodies locked together as if they were two halves of a single person. Her mouth opened and he felt her hot breath on his face. Her hands grasped his hips and drew him to an even tighter embrace.

"I want you," she whispered. "I want you so much, John Slocum."

"I want you, too, Velva," he said.

They roamed each other's bodies with their hands, and kissed with fire burning their lips, fire that fueled their desire for one another. He touched her firm breasts and twirled his fingers around the aureoles of her nipples. They hardened like young acorns and he kissed them, drew their nubs into his steaming mouth while Velva writhed in ecstasy.

"Now, now," she said, her voice almost hoarse.

"Not yet," he said, and traveled down her chest with his tongue blazing a hot trail to her tummy, and lower until his head was burrowed into her loins. Her back arched as if she were being pulled in two directions, from her head and her feet. She squirmed as his tongue plied the cleft of her vagina and laved the small clit that was the fountainhead of her passion.

Velva screamed softly as her fingernails clawed furrows in his back. Her body bucked as she surrendered to a sudden orgasmic spasm. She screamed and she sobbed with pleasure as he withdrew and covered her body with his.

She grasped his hard cock and pulled it to her portal. She spread her legs wide to receive him, and when the mushroomed crown of his cock entered her, she screamed again, softly, and mouthed a series of "oh, oh, ohs," as he plunged deeper into the steaming pudding of her cunt.

"You're so big," she breathed, and her body bucked once more as he pulled out and plunged inside her again with a thrust that took the breath from her lungs and incited her senses to a high-octave pitch. Feverishly, she moved her loins up and down, matching his thrusts with pelvic movements that took him so deep, his cock touched the wall of her womb and she spasmed with a series of rapid orgasms that oiled her lean body with sweat.

"Yes, yes, yes," she exclaimed and Slocum increased the rapidity of his plunging strokes, his tumescence stretching the skin of his member until it was as taut as a drumhead.

His thrusts took her to dizzying heights of ecstasy. She screamed softly each time she climaxed, and there seemed no end to her pleasure. She pulled on his buttocks and thrust her loins into his so that they were in perfect rhythm. He held back his own pleasure, wanting to please her, taking satisfaction that she was satisfied with him, with his vigorous way of making love.

"Oh, John, oh, John," she exclaimed. "It's so good, so gooood."

He slowed his strokes and let her languish on that rosy cloud floating above the earth. Then he gradually increased the speed of his pistoning thrusts until her eyes glazed, her mouth opened, and she gasped as a series of orgasms raked her senses, rippling through her lithe body like jolts of soft lightning. She slid her hands up to his back and dug her fingernails into his flesh. Her body bucked and thrashed beneath him.

"Now, now," she cooed.

Slocum drove into her. He felt the rush of pleasure course through his swollen, blood-engorged cock, and then, there was that moment when all his senses were blotted out. Velva screamed and his seed spurted into her womb, jetting warm and milky against the farthest wall of her vagina, splashing millions of seeds into every crevice in a steady stream.

John felt himself floating high above her, as if he had reached into the highest corner of the heavens where he experienced the thrill of creation itself, as if he had become a god in that one brilliant instant, no longer earthbound, but on some invisible summit where nothing mortal could touch him, a place where only angels dwelled.

She squeezed him tight against her and sighed a long sigh of deep satisfaction. They floated back to earth together, like two leaves in autumn, drifting down from dizzying peaks in a languorous lassitude that was as peaceful as a mountain glade in shadow.

"Ah," she said, "John, you man you. You took me places where I've never been."

"It was sweet, Velva," he said. "Very sweet."

"Oh, you don't know. You just don't know. You can't know."

"I know," he said.

"Only a woman could know," she said.

"I took pleasure in your pleasure," he said, his voice deep and husky.

He rolled off her and kissed one of her breasts. She reached down and grasped his softening manhood, held his organ gently in her hands.

Their bodies were oiled with sweat and her musk mingled with his manly scent, deepening their pleasure in the afterglow of their lovemaking.

"I suppose," she said after a time, when her breath had returned and they were both luxuriating in her bed, their bodies just touching, "you'd like to smoke."

"Why do you say that?" he asked.

"Don't all men desire a smoke after they've made love to a woman?"

"I suppose some men do."

"You smoke cheroots, don't you?"

"Yes."

"I'll get you one and light it for you."

"You don't have to do that," he said.

"Happy?" she asked as she slid out of bed.

"Yes. Very happy. You?"

"Supremely happy, John."

He watched her trip barefooted across the floor like some sylph-like creature, all curves and angles, a sprite of a woman, her skin glowing in the dim light of the sun's rays streaming through the window. She lifted his shirt and found his cheroots. She took one in hand and found his box of matches. She glided back to the bed, a smile on her face.

He opened his mouth and she placed the thin cigar between his lips. She struck a match and the smell of phosphorous stung his nostrils. He puffed and the end of the cheroot glowed as he drew its smoke into his lungs.

"We still have our drinks, too," she said. "Would you like a taste?"

"Umm," he said, rolling the cheroot from one side of his mouth to the other.

She laughed, and her laugh was girlish as she pranced to the bar and lifted their glasses. Slocum sat up and put a pillow behind his back. He saw an ashtray on the bedside table next to him. He tamped the ash from his smoke and laid the cheroot against the rim.

"Here's to a wonderful afternoon," she said. She handed him his glass and clinked hers against his.

"Yes," he said. "Wonderful."

She sat on the bed and drank. She looked at his nakedness with an admiring sweep of her eyes.

"You are some man, John Slocum."

He looked at her in frank admiration.

"And you're a woman to ride the river with, Velva. Truly."

"I'd ride anywhere with you," she said.

They drank. Slocum smoked and they saw the sun dropping low in the sky. Shadows striped the lawn outside her window. A quail piped from somewhere, its trill hanging in the air like the last notes of a minor symphony.

"Are you hungry?" she asked after a time.

"I could eat," he admitted.

"I'm famished."

"Let's eat then," he said.

They dined by candlelight on the veranda at the back of the house. Dusk brought a soft glow to the sky and seemed to linger as they ate and flirted with each other. They spoke with their eyes, and occasionally, she reached across the table and stroked the back of his hand. She wore a simple slip-on dress that clung to her body, all silken with a dull satiny sheen. His hair was still slightly tousled, and stubble sprouted from his jaw and chin.

Clarissa was invisible until they were finished eating. Then she appeared with a tray and set cups and saucers before them, cleared away their plates and utensils. She returned in moments with coffee steaming in a pot, a small pitcher of cream, and a bowl of sugar with a dainty spoon sticking out of it. She poured coffee into their cups and set an ashtray near Slocum. There were three wooden matchsticks inside the tray.

"Thank you, Clarissa," Slocum said.

She curtsied and smiled, then vanished into the kitchen as soundless as a bunny.

Velva laughed.

"I brought her over from Italy," she said.

"She's British?"

"Oh my, no. She's as American as you or I are. She traveled abroad and got stranded in Italy. She worked at a *pensione* and I discovered her, brought her back with me. She's a delightful companion and loves to keep house."

He lit a cheroot and sipped his coffee. The aroma was heady and it tasted faintly European. He supposed she had imported the coffee, too, but made no comment.

"I'm so happy, John," she said. "The funeral for Albert was dreadful and I was very low afterwards. And I was a little gloomy about coming home to an empty house. Even though Albert and I slept in separate rooms, he was something of a presence."

"I understand," he said. "You get used to someone."

"I couldn't stand to be around my husband," she said, "but he was like an old pair of shoes that were once comfortable and you hate to throw them out."

Slocum said nothing. He smoked and gazed out at the twilight, the soft contours of the mountains, the darkening trees.

"Will you stay the night?" she asked, changing the subject.

"I could," he said. "I have no good reason to go back to the hotel tonight."

"But do you want to stay?"

"Yes."

"I still want you, you know."

"Yes," he said. "I want you, too. Again."

His words brought a smile to her face and she stood up, walked around the table, and embraced him. She buried her face in his dark hair and drew his scent into her nostrils.

"Oh, your smell," she breathed. "It's better than wine. Better than French wine."

"That was good wine we had at supper," he said.

"It was a Bordeaux. It's almost as old as I am, I think."

They both laughed and he grasped her hand and kissed it.

"I could get used to you, John," she said. She glided away from him and walked to the railing on the veranda. The glow in the sky faded and the clouds turned ashen in the hush of evening.

Slocum did not say anything. He did not want to spoil the moment, nor dash her hopes.

But he was a man who did not settle, did not tarry long in any particular places. He was a rover and that was his nature. He had known many beautiful women, and he had taken much pleasure from them. But he had avoided rings and ceremonies, dollies and halters. He roamed free like the herds of buffalo, or the prowling panther.

He blew a smoke ring and watched it dance in the air like some ghostly doughnut. Then it wriggled free of its form and disintegrated into gray wisps that were like cobwebs blown to pieces by a hidden wind.

The land hushed and there was a deep silence between them. They lingered over their coffees and gazed into each other's eyes.

They both knew what was coming and were only waiting for night to draw them into its dark ocean like two mating seals on a deserted beach.

When they ascended the stairs, the house creaked with a dozen invisible clocks and they held each other's hands like children off on an adventurous lark. They entered the bedroom and Velva did not light a lamp. There was only the sound of their rustling clothes and the clatter of his boots to break the seemingly eternal silence.

10

Dave Jenner was sitting outside the hotel on one of the benches when Slocum rode up just after dawn. The sky was peach in the east and the last star was fading in the blue sky.

"Had breakfast yet, Slocum?" Jenner asked.

Slocum patted his belly and nodded.

"I've got grub in my saddlebags. Wondered if you wanted to take a little ride, do some trackin'?"

Jenner got up, squared his hat, and walked to the edge of the porch.

Slocum looked down at him, then at the hitchrail.

"I see two horses saddled here and a pair of mules loaded with panniers."

"That's Donnie's horse, and the pack mules."

"He's goin' with us?"

"Part of the deal I made with Mallory. He says he needs meat, and if you want your rent paid, you got to take Donnie up and bring back an elk."

"I could quit," Slocum said.

Jenner laughed.

"No need. We're just going to look around, follow them

63

horse tracks to that old camp. If that bunch is holed up there, you and Donnie can hunt elk and I'll come back and see if I can raise a posse."

"You have it all figured out, don't you, Dave?"

"You and I can't do much if that camp's full of Crow and hard cases. What do you call it in the Army? Take a look-see?"

"Reconnoiter," Slocum said.

Donnie came out of the hotel then, still chewing on something from breakfast. He wiped his mouth and grinned at Slocum.

"Daddy says we got to bring back an elk, Mr. Slocum."

"Did Sheriff Jenner tell you how dangerous it might be if you tag along with us?"

"Dangerous?"

"Yes, dangerous."

"I told Donnie we'd drop him off at a campsite of your choosing while you and I take a look at that place we talked about."

"Oh, I see," Slocum said. "It's kind of a two-pronged mission. Hunting two birds with one stone."

"We're just reconnoitering, remember?" Jenner said.

"What's 'reconnoiterin'?" Donnie asked.

"Never mind," Slocum said. He looked at Jenner.

"Let's go. Donnie, get on your horse and pull those two mules."

"Yes, sir," Donnie said. "I got saddlebags full of grub, candles, matches, a hatchet, and all kinds of stuff in case we have to stay up there a few nights."

Slocum drew a breath through his nostrils and bowed his head. Donnie scampered off the porch and untied the mules, held the rope, and climbed into his saddle. Jenner walked down the steps and mounted his horse.

"You missed a fine evening at the hotel, John," Jenner said as they rode down Main Street to the Billings Road.

"Them two gals gave a hell of a performance. The dining room was packed. Took folks' minds off of what happened yesterday."

"Some folks have short memories," Slocum said.

"By the way," Jenner said, "I got you a dozen cheroots at the general store yesterday. You owe me sixty cents."

"At that price, they must be made out of rope."

"Hemp, Slocum. I bought myself one and turned green when I smoked it."

Slocum laughed.

Donnie trailed along behind them, shivering in his light denim jacket. Cool air blew off the Yellowstone and the sky to the east was now a pale yellow, cloudless. Slocum had acclimated himself to the altitude, but his first days in Big Timber had brought mild headaches. Now he breathed the morning air with relish, filling his lungs with the dregs of the cool breeze that braced them.

"Them two gals looked all around for you last night. Jasmine wondered where you had gone."

"You tell her?" Slocum said.

"Nope. I told her you were probably worn down to a nub and asleep in your room. Why? Does it matter?"

"No, Dave. It doesn't matter."

"I think Mallory is going to hire them on. So they may be in town for a spell."

"I reckon we can handle a couple more belles in Big Timber."

"I'm worried about Jasmine's ex-husband, that Bruno feller. He might be more trouble than I can handle."

"He might. If he finds out she's working at the hotel, he might just show up there."

"I was thinkin' that. I could use them gals as bait to bring that bastard out in the open."

"Only thing is, Bruno's not alone. He's got him a gang of hard cases and some bloodthirsty Crow Indians."

"Yeah," Jenner said and kept silent for a time.

When they reached the site of the ambush, Jenner called a halt.

"What now, Slocum?" he asked.

Slocum turned to Donnie.

"Do you think you can find your way back to where we kept the mules, by that cave?"

"I think so," Donnie said. "I just ride on up that wood-cutters' road to where we found the Lorraines and their manager, then up the opposite slope."

"Above that bluff where we kept the mules, there's a flat place, with trees and a little spring-fed stream. Make camp there and wait for me. I should be there before sunset. Can you do that, Donnie?"

"I sure can," he said with a wide grin on his face.

"I don't want you to leave that place. Don't hunt elk, and if you see any, don't shoot them. Understand?"

"Sure, I understand," Donnie said.

"Whatever you do, just stay put up behind that bluff where the cave is. I mean it."

"I'll do just what you say, Mr. Slocum."

"If you don't," Jenner said, "you might get killed."

Donnie's eyes widened and he swallowed. He looked a little sickly for a moment.

He waved good-bye to the two men and started up the old logging road, pulling the mules behind him. He did not look back.

"I'm glad that's over," Jenner said. "I know you have to make meat for Mallory and he's tied that albatross of a kid around your neck. The kid just doesn't look right to me."

"He's all right. Just young. Let's get to the job you and I have in front of us."

Donnie disappeared from sight and Jenner heaved a sigh.

Jenner and Slocum rode up the slight ridge and into the timber. They went past the place where the Crow and Bruno had waited to bushwhack the coach and wagons.

"That soft soil made the tracks easy to follow," Jenner said.

"Yes, but you know where that old camp is, right?"

"I have a general idea. We'll follow the tracks up the mountain, and when I think we're getting near that place, we'll turn off and come up parallel to it. We don't want to ride right up on where they're stayin'."

Slocum nodded.

"Lead the way," he said.

Jenner ticked his horse in its flanks and they scrambled up on the small ridge. They followed the tracks that went both ways. The trail led through deadfalls and past elk wallows and deer trails. Jays flitted among the spruce and pines like fluttering blue lights, chirping but not squawking.

The sun rose higher in the sky and shot rays through the timber, lighting up small glades and moving shadows around like chess pieces.

They topped one foothill, then another. The riders they tracked had taken the easiest path from a higher elevation, skirting rocky outcroppings, riding around large deadfalls where mighty pines had toppled.

The two men did not speak. They rode slowly through the tall timber and tried not to make noise. At one point, they heard noises and stopped. Three antlerless elk arose from wallows and lumbered off through the trees. They watched them go without comment. But they were both thinking the same thing. Slocum could have killed one of them, dressed it out, and taken the meat back to the hotel.

An hour passed, then another.

Jenner reined up and waited for Slocum to come alongside.

"I think that old camp is over the next rise," Jenner whispered.

Slocum looked up. The slope was steep. Mountain peaks rose behind it, some snowcapped. It was hard to tell if there was a plateau beyond the rise, but he had seen such places before in the high Rockies.

"We better start making a circle," Slocum said, his voice barely audible.

"Split up?" Jenner said.

"No. If we see anything, we need to see it together."

"I agree."

"You need to figure out how big that camp is and how far we have to ride to flank it."

"I think I can do that," Jenner said.

They rode in a straight line parallel to the ridge that they deemed to be above them. It was rough going, with deep gullies and fallen trees they had to circumvent. Rocky outcroppings that looked like the ruins of ancient cities blocked their path at times. The horses clawed their way up steep grades that were still soft from melted spring snow, and in shadowed places, white snow glistened like ermine pelts.

The air was thin and cool. Slocum figured they must be about 10,000 or 11,000 feet above sea level. When he looked up at the peaks, he could see where the timberline was, where gray granite began.

They jumped a young mule deer, watched it gallop downhill at an angle, its hooves flying, its tail a dim flag as it bounded between the fir and spruce, the tall pines.

Finally, Jenner turned his horse and they began to climb again. They cleared the ridge and saw that they were on a shelf, a plateau, dotted with trees. Chipmunks scuttled away from them and dove into burrows. Partridges took flight or ran for cover, their gray bodies fat, their wings covered with dust.

Beyond the plateau, they saw the flat granite shape of limestone bluffs. Water seeped from rifts and fissures in the rock, and there was a small creek that ran parallel to the lofty mountains beyond.

Jenner stopped and looked off down the flat.

"Look familiar?" Slocum whispered.

"Somewhat. I think that camp is yonder. This plateau

widens out. I remember the flat was pretty wide, better'n a quarter mile."

"Maybe we ought to tie up our horses over in the pines and proceed on foot."

"I think you're right, Slocum. It could be just beyond that clump of juniper and spruce trees, or another mile or two."

"We can walk it," Slocum said.

They rode a short distance, then dismounted. They concealed their horses in a small grove of bushy firs and spruce, tied them to juniper bushes. They slid their rifles from their sheaths. Jenner reached into his saddlebag and pulled out two sandwiches wrapped in brown paper. He handed one to Slocum.

"You want to carry your canteen?"

Slocum shook his head.

"Too noisy. We got a little creek here if we get real thirsty."

He stuffed his sandwich inside his shirt. Jenner did the same.

The two men walked along the bluff, through scraggly pines and thickets of alder bushes. They stopped every few minutes to listen. They made little noise, and what noise they did make was drowned out by the burble of the small creek as it coursed its way over worn pebbles and fallen rocks.

After a time, when they stopped, they heard voices. Men's voices. They listened, but neither could make out the words. They moved closer, crouched over, each step careful and slow.

They came to a place where there was a game trail leading upward from the flat. It was grassy and gradual. Jenner stopped and gestured toward it.

Slocum nodded.

They left the plateau and climbed carefully up the sloping game trail as wide as a wagon. Then they followed a well-worn path along the top of the bluff.

Jenner stopped and pointed downward.

Slocum craned his neck and saw the outline of a log cabin.

It was very quiet and the voices had gone silent.

The two men waited.

And listened.

It seemed an eternity before they heard a man say something.

"About time them Injuns was gettin' back here, Bruno, don't you think?"

"Don't you worry none, Jake," a man with a deep voice said, "them Crow know what they're doin'."

Slocum froze. Ice streamed down his spine.

He knew that voice.

He had heard it before.

And he knew where he had heard it.

His eyes narrowed and his jaw hardened to iron.

Jenner looked at him, his eyebrows arched, wrinkles rippling above his nose.

Slocum's lips tightened and he lay flat, crawled to the edge of the bluff.

He saw the man whose voice he had heard. The one the other man had called Bruno.

He felt his stomach churn, the muscles of his abdomen quiver.

Yes, he thought, that was the man.

Only Slocum knew him by a different name.

11

Slocum stared down at the man he believed to be Bruno Valenti.

That was not the name Slocum knew him by, but the two had met.

Jenner scooted close to Slocum and looked over the edge of the precipice. Then he tapped Slocum on the shoulder and held up both hands in a gesture of helplessness, or ignorance.

Slocum put a finger to his lips to indicate silence, then cupped one ear.

The two men listened to the conversation between Valenti and one of his cohorts. Their voices floated upward and were quite audible in the thin mountain air.

"You got to learn one thing, Pettibone," Valenti said. "Patience. You got to be patient."

"Hell, I'm as patient as the next man, Bruno. I was just askin' is all."

"Well, them Crow is doin' one thing and I sent Crowley to do another."

"I don't trust them damned Injuns," Pettibone said. He

had a wad of chewing tobacco in his mouth, and spat a stream of brown liquid onto a nearby rock. It splatted and left an oozing stain. Pettibone, like Valenti, hadn't touched a razor to his face for at least three days and his chin was mottled with the shadow of an emerging beard.

Valenti wore a hat, like Pettibone, but his hair was long and curly, black as a raven's wing. He wasn't tall, but he had round muscular shoulders that tautened his faded chambray shirt, and powerful hairy arms that jutted from rolled-up sleeves. His boots, like Pettibone's, were covered in dust, but the polish was dull underneath and nearly all gone from the leather.

Slocum scanned the small cluster of log cabins. They were arranged in a semicircle, at least one hundred yards apart. There was a lean-to at one end of the mesa, a large one, where horses were tied. Slocum recognized the horses and his jaw hardened when he saw them. He couldn't make out the brands from that distance, but he knew what they were. The cabins all had low ceilings and heavy split-log doors. They were weathered and he could see gaps where the chinking had disintegrated. There was grass growing on the plateau and he saw mounds of bones, and leftover food had been tossed to rot and decay. He saw trenches where the men had relieved themselves, and there were posts erected to hang game they had killed so that the animals could be skinned, bled, and quartered for their sustenance. There was a smell to the place that was both old and new. Men were living on that flat ridge where men had lived before.

At the other end of the mesa, near a stand of pines and spruce, three teepees stood, their poles jutting from the unpainted and undecorated deerskin lodges.

"You don't need to trust them Injuns, Jake. They're hungry as wolves and I give 'em just enough firewater to keep them loyal to me."

"Well, I can't see wastin' good whiskey on a bunch of redskins. We don't have that much for ourselves."

"That's going to be taken care of," Valenti said.

"How? We goin' back to Billings and buy whiskey and goods?"

"No, we're not. The little town of Big Timber has all we need. Soon as Harry Wicks gets back, I'll tell everybody my plan."

"So, you got a plan, eh, Bruno? I mean 'sides them two women you're tryin' to grab."

"You're damned right I got a plan, Jake," Valenti said. "Had it for a good long time."

"I sure as hell can hardly wait to hear what it is. I don't like livin' up here with Injuns and no women or a soft bed."

"We won't be here long," Valenti said. He got up and walked to the nearest cabin. Jake Pettibone spit and walked over to one of the trenches to relieve himself.

Slocum scooted backward, slowly and silently. A moment later, Jenner did the same. When they were both some distance from the edge of the precipice, they stood up and walked to a copse of blue spruce.

"You got something to tell me, John?" Jenner asked.

"Valenti. I met him in Billings. Only he went by the name of George Colby."

"You did? Did you know—"

Slocum didn't let Dave finish his sentence.

"I sold him six horses. I met him in Kansas City. He told me his name was George Colby and he wanted six horses with Arab blood in them. Said he was going to hunt mountain lions in Montana. Wanted horses that were surefooted with small hooves. He paid me half the money in advance, told me to bring them to Billings. He said he'd be in the Antlers Hotel there. And so he was. He paid me in full and I forgot all about it."

"There's got to be more to it than that. How did you wind up in Big Timber?"

Slocum detected a note of suspicion in Jenner's voice.

"After I delivered the horses, we had a drink in the hotel

bar. I asked him about hunting mountain lions and he said there were guides in Big Timber and that it was a town that catered to hunters."

"So you just rode up to Big Timber and started hunting for Mallory."

"Not exactly. There was an ad in the Billings newspaper for a meat hunter. I applied for the job and got it. That satisfy you?"

"Jake Pettibone. Did you meet him in Billings? Do you know the man?"

"Nope. I just met Bruno Valenti there, who called himself George Colby."

"And he didn't mention the name of Pettibone?"

"Nope. He said he had some hunting partners, from back East, I think he said. Why?"

"Because," Jenner said, "I've got a dodger in my office with that man's likeness on it. There's a two-hundred-dollar reward for his capture."

"So, he's an outlaw. That shouldn't surprise you."

"He's a murderer, John. He killed a family in Saint Louis, robbed a bank in Denver with three other men who are also wanted."

"I'll be damned," Slocum said.

They walked back to where they had left their horses.

"If my hunch is right, John, Valenti not only has Pettibone, but those other three. They robbed a bank in Denver and killed the banker, a male teller, and a female secretary. U.S. marshals are huntin' them, and they might be right here under our noses."

"Seems like Valenti has some kind of plan that involves not only the Lorraines, but Big Timber."

"I got to get me a posse and talk to our banker there. Frankly, John, I'm scared shitless."

"What are you going to do, Dave?"

"I'm going back up there and see what I can find out,

then go back to town in the morning and start making plans of my own."

"You better make sure you don't get caught up here. Those Crow can smell you."

"I'm going to wallow in pine boughs and rub sap on my face and hands. That'll kill my scent."

"Good luck," Slocum said.

"You goin' off to meet up with Donnie?"

"I'm going to get an elk and take it to the hotel. I'll see you in town."

"When?"

"Sometime tomorrow, I reckon."

"Elk are in the high meadows this time of year."

Slocum laughed.

"And that's just where I told Donnie to make camp."

Slocum climbed into the saddle and rode off. Jenner started walking back to where they had overheard Valenti and Pettibone talking.

Slocum rode to a ridge above where the outlaw camp was and dropped down into a small valley, heading toward the place he had told Donnie to go. He traveled by dead reckoning, using the mountain peaks as his guide.

He thought about Valenti and how their paths had crossed. It seemed a strange twist of fate that he had provided the horses Bruno and his outlaw henchmen were riding. And now he knew Jasmine and Lydia and the danger they were in from Valenti. It made his skin crawl to think of what Bruno and his men had done, and that they were riding horses he had sold to them.

Fate, he decided, was also full of ironies.

And maybe Fate had decreed that he and the man he had known as George Colby would meet again.

Would that be Fate? Or Destiny?

He wondered.

12

Slocum ate the sandwich Jenner had given him on the ride through the timber. He washed the food down with swallows of water from a nearby stream. It was midafternoon when he rode a game trail down into the meadow where he had told Donnie to make camp. He had, on his ride through the timber, seen a lot of elk and mule deer sign, and the game trail was a maze of cuneiform impressions of deer and elk hooves that a blind man could decipher.

He could smell the musk, not only of deer and elk, but of bear scat mingled with the heady scent of fragrant pines. He heard Donnie's horse whicker and spotted the mules when he reached the flat. Donnie stepped out of a cluster of pines and raised an arm to wave at Slocum.

There were no visible signs of a camp and Slocum nodded in approval as he approached.

He dismounted, stuck the index finger of his right hand in his mouth, covering it with saliva. He held it up and felt the breeze blow on his wet finger.

"You did well, Donnie, making camp downwind of that game trail."

"What game trail?"

"The one I rode down. You didn't see it?"

"No, I been sitting back there in the trees just a-listenin'. I think I heard some elk up above me on that next ridge."

"You probably did," Slocum said. "I expect we can find elk if we put our minds to it."

"I'm plumb ready. My trigger finger's been itchin' somethin' fierce all day."

"You didn't load your rifle, did you?"

"No, sir, but I got me a cartridge in my pocket ready to slide into the magazine."

"Hold your horses, Donnie. I'll tell you when to load that cartridge. Let's see the camp."

Donnie led Slocum into the pines to a small clearing, where he had laid out his bedroll. His rifle lay atop it. He had gathered stones, dug a small pit, and ringed it with the rocks. He had also gathered dead limbs and chopped the kindling with a small hatchet, which now leaned against a small pine.

"Nice camp, Donnie," Slocum said. "Now, let's hunt us down an elk while the sun's still up."

Donnie picked up his rifle.

"Do we ride or walk?" he asked.

"Ride. It's pretty steep up there and elk can move fast. You just follow me. If we jump one or two or three, we just might get lucky."

"I'll saddle my horse," Donnie said. "Did you and the sheriff find the outlaw camp?"

"We did," Slocum said.

"I got a hunnert questions for you about that," Donnie said as threw a saddle blanket on his horse.

"Don't ask," Slocum said.

Donnie saddled his horse in a sulking silence. Slocum climbed into the saddle and looked up at the sky. There was still plenty of daylight left and he suspected the timber was full of elk. They would be bedded down at that time of day and they ought to jump a few if they were careful. Elk did not seem to fear horses, but if they smelled a human, they would run from the scent.

They rode back up the game trail and Slocum told Donnie to look down at all the tracks.

"Don't say anything, Donnie," he said. "Just look."

Slocum left the trail following spoor through the timber. He pointed out the tracks, the overturned stones, the crushed pine needles, the broken limbs where elk had stepped. He just pointed and hoped Donnie would know what to look for if he ever hunted on his own. This was part of his bargain with Ray Mallory. He not only had to bring fresh game to the hotel, but had to teach Ray's kid how to hunt elk and deer.

Slocum followed tracks, then veered off into heavy timber where the going was rougher. They had to ride around huge pines that had toppled and were rotting, avoid rocky outcroppings that blocked their way. But this was where the elk felt most at home. The pines were thick and grew close together. His line of sight was considerably shortened, but they did come across a fresh wallow where three elk had been bedding down only moments before.

Slocum knew Donnie was excited, but he turned to him and put a finger to his lips to indicate silence. Donnie nodded.

They halted and Slocum sat there for a long while just listening. He turned his head to pick up any sound.

Finally, they heard a heavy footfall in the timber above them.

Slocum held up his hand to gesture that Donnie should not move. He was sure that the lad had heard the same sound because Donnie was looking in the same direction as Slocum was.

It was quiet for a few moments, then they heard the sound of an elk breaking dried pine limbs. It was above them, on a parallel course.

Slocum looked but he didn't see the animal, and the animal probably could not see him. The wind was blowing against his face, so he figured the elk had not picked up their scent.

He prodded Ferro and the horse stepped out. Slocum guided him to a slightly higher elevation and kept heading into the breeze that blew down from above them.

Donnie followed him at the same slow pace.

Slocum reined up and held up a hand to halt Donnie.

They listened.

It was quiet for several moments and then they heard heavy footfalls not far away. Slocum peered through the timber and saw a pair of large brown legs. Then he saw an ear and, a second or two later, a yellowish rump.

He mentally gauged the yardage.

The elk was about fifty or sixty yards above them. It was moving slow. It was eating something, grass or blackberries, succulent leaves from a bush. Now it was making a lot of noise.

But it was hard to see the animal. There was a lot of brush, and the trees were thick.

Slocum waited and watched. The elk seemed unperturbed. It was feeding and oblivious to the fact that it was being watched.

He gestured to Donnie to ride up alongside him. He pointed to the feeding elk, a large heavy cow, he figured. Donnie craned his neck and watched as the elk moved out of their line of sight. But they could still hear it every time it moved. It was on a path of its choosing, and Slocum wanted it to move well away from them, well out of earshot.

Finally, when the sounds of the elk faded into silence, Slocum leaned over to speak to Donnie.

"Get your rifle," he whispered. "Move the bolt real slow so you don't make much noise. Don't cock it."

Donnie nodded and slowly slid his rifle out of its scabbard.

Slocum pulled his Winchester '74 from its sheath. He waited until Donnie had loaded his rifle and then worked the lever action, injecting a cartridge into the firing chamber. He closed the action and laid the rifle across his lap.

Donnie looked at him, a questioning look on his face.

Slocum leaned over again and whispered into Donnie's ear.

"I'm going to ride up and get on that elk's track. We'll take it real slow. You ride on this same course and stop every so often to listen. I'll do the same."

Donnie craned his neck over and whispered to Slocum, "If I see it, do I shoot it?"

Slocum considered the question.

"If the elk sees us or smells us, it will probably run to higher ground. If you get a shot, take it."

Donnie beamed.

"Wait until I give you the sign to ride," Slocum whispered.

Then he turned Ferro and slowly ascended the slope until he found the path the elk had taken. The cow was munching on leaves and tufts of grass. Its hoofprints were deep in the soft damp soil. It was easy to track.

Slocum rode slowly ahead until he was slightly forward of where Donnie sat his horse. Then he looked down and lifted his hand and nodded.

Donnie proceeded on the same track he and Slocum had been following. He looked up at Slocum every now and then to make sure he wasn't getting ahead of him. When Slocum stopped, Donnie stopped.

Ferro followed the spoor, sniffing at the elk scent and stepping slow because Slocum held a tight rein on him. They advanced, and the trail led around heavy clumps of brush and a rocky outcropping.

Less than a half hour later, Slocum spotted the tallow rump of the elk. Its head was down as it fed and it was not lifting it to sniff the air. He and Ferro crept closer. Slocum pointed ahead so Donnie would be on the lookout.

Slocum closed the distance, and when the elk was about fifty yards away, he stopped and put the rifle to his shoulder.

He motioned for Donnie to keep riding forward.

When he saw that Donnie was directly parallel to the elk, Slocum held the trigger and cocked the hammer back on his rifle. The click was muffled, barely audible.

Then he saw Donnie rein in his horse and put his rifle to his shoulder.

Slocum waited. All he could see was the elk's rump and part of its side.

He watched as Donnie sighted down the barrel of his single-shot, bolt-action rifle.

Donnie fired.

The explosion echoed off the rocks. The elk jumped and Slocum had a clear shot at its heart. He held his breath and squeezed the trigger. The rifle bucked against his shoulder. Sparks and lead flew from the barrel. He heard a smack and saw the elk stagger. He jacked another cartridge into the chamber and nudged Ferro forward.

Donnie ejected his empty hull and put another round in the chamber of his rifle.

"I got him," Donnie shouted.

He spurred his horse and started up the slope.

The elk thrashed in the brush. Slocum saw gouts of blood on the ground, and the surrounding leaves were spattered with red droplets.

He reached the dying elk first. It lifted its head, but there was a hole right behind its left leg. Blood spurted from its mouth and nostrils. The animal moaned in mortal agony.

Donnie rode up.

Slocum drew his six-gun, cocked it, and fired a round into the elk's head. It kicked its hind legs in a spasmodic jerk and lay still. The blood stopped oozing from the hole in its side.

There was another hole in the elk, just under its spine.

Donnie's shot.

"I got him, I got him," Donnie exclaimed excitedly.

"You sure did, Donnie."

"Hot damn."

Slocum shoved his rifle back in its boot, dismounted, and ground-tied Ferro to a sturdy bush. Donnie climbed out of the saddle. He laid his gun against a tree and stared down at the dead elk.

"That's the easy part of hunting," Slocum said. "Now comes the hard part."

"What's that?"

"Dressing the cow out and packing the meat down to camp."

"I don't know how to do none of that," Donnie said.

"Then you just watch."

Slocum drew his knife from his stovepipe boot and kneeled over the cow. He spread its front legs and sliced a deep cut from its throat, down its belly, to the anus. Donnie recoiled as the guts were exposed and a cloud of steam, odorous as an outhouse hole, issued from the bowels of the animal.

Donnie's eyes rolled in their sockets and his legs crumpled.

Slocum started pulling intestines and organs from the cow's stomach.

Donnie staggered away a few feet and fainted. He hit the ground with a thud.

Slocum chuckled to himself and continued to dress out the elk with his big knife.

Donnie lay facedown, dead to the world.

Flies zizzed around the entrails, and a jay flitted to a nearby pine limb and started a raucous squawking. Other jays flew to nearby trees and blared their calls through the timber.

Slocum smiled.

He had meat for Mallory's hotel guests and he felt good. It had taken three bullets to get the elk, but they had gotten it.

The horses looked on as Slocum continued to cut away the front legs and the cow's head.

Finally, the jays flew away and the mountains were silent, their snowcapped peaks shining brilliant white in the blaze of the afternoon sun.

13

Adolph Gruenig, the lone butcher in Big Timber, smacked his lips when he saw the elk meat Slocum and Donnie carried into his shop. It was close to dusk when they got there, and Gruenig had already lit a lamp.

"Oh, *das ist gut,*" he exclaimed. "*Herr* Mallory will be pleased. I will cut up the meat tonight, *ja,* and you come for some of it in the morning, Donnie."

"I will, Mr. Gruenig," Donnie said. "Thanks."

"You tell your papa I make de good cuts. So much meat, eh."

Slocum and Donnie rode to the livery. Slocum put Ferro in his stall and put grain in his feed bin, saw to it that he had water in his trough. Donnie put his horse up and the mules he turned outside in the corral. The stableman, Wilbur Snead, was at supper. Donnie and Slocum walked back to the hotel. They looked at the raw sky beyond the high peaks of the mountains. It was as red as barn paint behind the gilded clouds that were already fading to an ashen hue. By the time they reached the hotel, the last rays of sunlight were falling into the horizon like spent fireworks.

"I'll tell Pop what Mr. Gruenig said, Mr. Slocum. See you tomorrow?"

"I'm not sure," Slocum said. "Don't plan on it. I expect Sheriff Jenner will have me busy."

"Is he back yet?"

"I don't know."

Slocum got his key from the clerk, the austere Alfred Duggins, who did not speak to him, as if Slocum were an inferior. As he passed the desk, he saw the large poster on an easel.

APPEARING TONIGHT
THE LORRAINES
MOTHER AND DAUGHTER
IN THE DINING SALON
8:00 P.M.

Slocum carried his bedroll, saddlebags, and rifle to his room on the second floor. He entered and walked to the highboy, where he kept a bottle of Kentucky bourbon on a tray, with two upside-down glasses and a pitcher of water. He threw his gear on the bed as he passed it. He poured himself a generous glass of whiskey and filled the other tumbler with water.

He carried the glasses to the small table in the center of the room and sat down. He stretched his long legs out straight and drank a sip of the whiskey. It tasted good. He was grimy from dressing out the elk and sweating in the sun on the way back to Big Timber.

He drank the whiskey, then bathed himself with a wash-cloth, soap, and water, then changed clothes. He had just finished the buff on his boots when there was a knock on his door. He threw down the polishing cloth and strode to the door.

"Who is it?" he said.

"Ray Mallory."

He opened the door and there stood the hotel owner holding a piece of paper in his hand.

"Come on in, Ray," Slocum said.

"Got yourself all cleaned up, I see. We have a bathhouse, you know. Out back. Hot water, soap, towels."

"I know. Have a seat."

"This message was left at the desk for you. I saved Alfred a trip since I wanted to talk to you."

Mallory handed Slocum the note. He walked to the table and sat down, looked at the bottle of whiskey, the two glasses.

"I must remember to have the maid bring you some extra glasses," he said.

Slocum opened the note.

"John," it read, "can you meet me in my office tonight? Say about 6:30 or 7:00. Urgent."

The note was signed: "David Jenner, Sheriff of Big Timber."

"You know what's in the note?" Slocum said.

"Of course. Dave sent a man over from his office. I was there when it was delivered."

"Some people would say that was snoopy."

"The note was not folded over. I couldn't help but read it. Also, the man who delivered it went to see a man staying here at my hotel and asked him to see Sheriff Jenner. Something about a posse."

"You don't miss much, do you, Ray?"

"Big Timber's a small town. Not much goes on here that I don't know about."

"Donnie told you we dropped some elk meat off at the butcher shop?"

"That's why I came up to see you. I want to thank you for taking Donnie under your wing. He was very excited about killing that big elk. He said you let him shoot it."

Slocum said nothing.

"I just wanted you to know how grateful I am. There's a

big change in that boy. You gave him a chance to become a man."

"He's all right," Slocum said.

"You can pick up your pay in the morning at the desk. There's a little extra in it to show my gratitude."

"That was our deal, Ray. Take Donnie hunting and show him the ropes."

"Yes, but I never thought he could shoot an elk all by himself practically his first time out."

"I don't know when I'll be able to take him hunting again. I have a hunch Jenner's going to need help."

"What did you two find out?" Mallory asked.

"I'll let the sheriff give you that information, Ray. He may want to keep a lid on it for a time."

"I understand, John."

Mallory drew his watch out of his watch pocket. It was on a chain.

"Well, it's getting close to six thirty, John. I don't want to keep you."

"I'll walk over and see what Dave has to say."

Mallory stood up.

"I hope Dave can bring those scoundrels to justice who ambushed the stage and killed all those people."

"I do, too," Slocum said.

Mallory walked toward the door. Then he stopped and turned around.

"I'm grateful to you, also, John, for bringing the Lorraines to my hotel. They are quite an attraction."

"You've hired them on?"

"For a month, at least. I am sending flyers to Billings, Livingston, and every town along the Yellowstone and the Gallatin. Their manager helped me with the advertisement."

"Don't thank me, Ray. They wanted to stay here."

"Yes, but you made sure they did and I'm mighty pleased about it."

Mallory left and Slocum strapped on his gun belt, put on his hat.

The sky over the mountains was the color of a dove's breast, and some of the streetlamps were lit when he walked to Sheriff Jenner's office. There were horses outside, reins wrapped around the hitchrail.

When he walked in, Dave was standing in front of three men who had their right hands raised.

"I hereby deputize you men," Dave said.

The men put their hands down.

"Be here at sunup tomorrow," Dave said. He let them out without introducing them to Slocum. He closed and locked the door behind them. Then he pulled the shades.

As he stepped to his desk, he blocked the lamplight and became a shadowy silhouette. He sat down and waved Slocum to a chair.

"I see you got yourself a posse, Dave," Slocum said.

"Three pissants," Jenner said.

"Best you could do, I reckon."

"I sent a telegram to the U.S. marshal in Helena when I got back. He should have it by morning. Not in time to help us, but I told him we were dealing with some pretty bad hombres and a handful of scalping Crow braves."

"Maybe you should have called out the U.S. Army, Dave."

"Yeah. That would take a least a month, maybe two."

"Well, what's your plan?"

Slocum tilted his hat back on his head and stretched out his legs.

"That's why I wanted you to come over. John, I'm scared shitless."

Jenner picked up a stack of wanted dodgers and held them out.

"Every one of those men up there at that camp has a price on his head."

"So?"

"I got all their names, and if you read these, you'll know I'm dealing with cold-blooded killers. And even with those I just swore in, and you, I don't think I can stop 'em."

"Do you know what Valenti is planning to do?"

"I've got some of it. He wants those women pretty bad."

"The Lorraines?"

"Yes. But he's got something else in mind and that's what scares me."

"What else?"

Jenner dropped the flyers and leaned across the desk.

"I don't know. Valenti's keeping his men in the dark. But we've got to get that mother and her daughter out of town, put 'em in a safe place."

"When?"

"Tonight, if we can. John, I need your help on this. There's no time to waste."

Slocum pulled a cheroot out of his pocket. He didn't light it. He just looked at Jenner and felt a tinge of sadness.

Jenner was in over his head. He would need more than his help to get Jasmine and Lydia to leave Big Timber. There was desperation in Jenner's eyes. He looked, Slocum thought, like a man who had just been sentenced to die on the gallows.

14

Harry Wicks was one of those men who might be called nondescript. People seldom noticed him. When he was in a town, or part of a crowd, he was one who always escaped notice. He had no distinguishing facial features. He was quiet and deceptive.

Those characteristics were what made Wicks a valuable accomplice when outlaws needed a lookout or someone to blend in when a robbery was planned.

Wicks was the man Bruno Valenti sent into Big Timber after the attack on the stagecoach and wagons. He was the man who could garner the information Valenti needed without being noticed at all.

And Harry Wicks was also a very observant man. He was so anonymous that his face had never appeared on a wanted dodger or was ever mentioned by eyewitnesses who had been his victims.

So when he rode into the old camp, Valenti was anxious to hear what he had to say.

It was late afternoon when the Crow braves returned. They had killed three sheep. They had dressed them out and packed the meat in the hides, which served as bundles.

Valenti, Pettibone, and the others in Bruno's band watched the Crow braves ride in and almost missed seeing Wicks, who was riding right behind them. They only noticed him because he was white and wearing white man's clothing. But at first, they only saw the Crow, who were also wearing white man's clothes. They were riding paints. Wicks was riding a cow pony with patches of white hair in its otherwise brown hide. So he escaped notice, even among his brethren.

"Ain't that Harry?" Pettibone said as the Crow rode single file toward their teepees.

"Yep, that's Harry, right at the tail end of them Injuns," Angus Macgregor said. "Damned if he don't look half-Crow on that pony."

Valenti laughed.

"That's why I sent him into Big Timber," Bruno said. "The man's like a leaf on a tree full of leaves. He don't stand out like the rest of you ugly bastards."

Jim Cochran snorted and self-consciously touched a hand to his bearded face as if to confirm or deny Valenti's comment about his looks. Cochran had red hair that was thinning so that it looked like strands of copper wire streaming across the bald spot in the middle of his skull. He was short and stocky and stood out, even in that group of hard cases, like a boiled thumb.

"Well, Harry," Valenti said when Wicks rode up and dismounted, "what did you find out?"

Wicks handed the reins of his horse to Pettibone.

"Your gal and her daughter are stayin' at the Big Timber Hotel. Singin' there, as a matter of fact."

"What about that little weasel, Fenster?"

"He's with 'em. I think them gals will be singin' in the dining salon ever' night for a while."

"What about the bank?"

"It's a pushover, Bruno. They got one gal teller and one shrimp of a man. Banker's office is right behind the cages.

They got a vault and leave it open most of the time."

"No guard?"

"No guard. It's a little old bank, kind of like a post of-fice."

"But they got money," Valenti said.

"They seem to be doin' business. A lot of people came in and put money on the counter."

"Good. We can kill two birds with one stone," Valenti said.

"The gals is up on the second floor. Room 122. Fenster is lodged in Room 124, right next door."

"We can sure put that jasper's lights out if he interferes," Valenti said.

The Crow were skinning out the sheep. One of them walked over to where Valenti and his men were sitting around a campfire that had been built, but was unlit.

"Here comes Two Knives," Cochran said.

Valenti raised his head and looked at the approaching Crow.

"*Hau*," Two Knives said. "Kill sheep." He held up three fingers, then rubbed his belly. "Good meat. You cook."

"You eat with us, Two Knives. You and your braves. You done good."

"Heap good," Two Knives said. He was a stoical man, unsmiling, with piercing brown eyes that looked black, and long black hair braided into a single pigtail that was tucked inside his thin muslin shirt. He wore rumpled trousers that were slightly too large for him. His belt was a piece of rough hemp rope. He wore a knife and a small .38 caliber pistol in a worn holster. His beaded headband protruded from under his battered felt hat, which bore the stains of many a meal.

"Me and the boys will be leavin' camp in a day or two," Valenti said. He signed, swirling a circle to include the group of white men, straddling a finger with two on the other hand, making a crude fork. Then, the sign for go and showing one sun to indicate the day they would be gone. "You stay here. Wait."

"Two Knives no go?"

Valenti shook his head.

"If you go with us," he said, "many soldiers come. They hunt you. Take you back to Agency."

Two Knives grunted.

He and his men had sneaked away from the Crow Agency in Wyoming with Valenti's help. They wanted money to buy rifles and bullets, which Valenti had promised them.

"You go," Two Knives said. "We wait. We hunt. We eat."

Valenti grinned.

"We bring money. Buy guns. Guns for you and your braves."

"Good," Two Knives said. He walked back to his camp. He was slightly bowlegged and rocked from side to side as he walked.

"You give them redskins guns, Bruno, we'll all lose our scalps," Cochran said.

"You let me worry about that."

"Well, what about that bank in Big Timber?" Pettibone said. "When do we clean it out?"

"Next stage is due on Saturday. Two days from now. I reckon they'll bring money from Billings for that bank. Ain't that right, Harry?"

"Yep. Bank sends a clerk to the stage stop to pick up a big bag."

Wicks had spent two weeks in Big Timber. He hadn't been present when the gang ambushed the stage. The Monday stage, which carried no money.

"So late afternoon, the bank should have the money, right?"

"They will," Wicks said. "They count it after the bank closes. So it'll still be in that bag."

"Mighty convenient," Cochran said, a wry grin on his sun-freckled face.

"Harry and Jake will go to the hotel and get Jasmine and Lydia. I want 'em both, but if they only get Jasmine, that'll be all right. The rest of us will be withdrawing money from the Big Timber Bank right at closing time. We'll all meet there."

"What about the sheriff?" Cochran asked.

Valenti looked at Wicks for an answer.

"He ain't much, and he ain't got no deputies. We can take him down with one shot from a Greener if he butts in."

"That answer your question, Cochran?" Valenti said.

"Macgregor, you'll be on the street outside the bank. You keep an eye on the hotel and for that sheriff." Valenti stood up and stretched.

"Glad to be of service," Macgregor said.

"I'll give you the final details on Saturday morning," Valenti said.

He looked at his men. They all nodded in agreement.

"Now, let's get that fire started and break out the fry pans. I could eat a southbound horse headin' north."

The men scattered, each to his own task. Cochran struck a match and touched it to the squaw wood they had gathered to put beneath the kindling. The flames spread fast and the squaw wood crackled.

The sun lit the distant peaks, turning their snowy tips to a golden radiance. Jays perched on the roofs of the log cabins, watching the activity in the camp. Some distance away, buzzards circled in the sky on invisible carousels and wolves gulped down the innards of the dead elk, snarling at the swarm of flies that attacked all the bloody parts.

The Crow cut up the mutton. One or two scraped the hides and fashioned willow withes for curing. They looked over at the fire and grunted their approval.

They, too, were hungry.

15

Slocum and Jenner were surprised when someone began pounding on the sheriff's door. Dusk's gray shadows seeped through the edges of the pulled shades.

"I wonder who that could be," Jenner said. He arose from his chair, walked to the door, lifted the latch, and opened it.

Slocum saw a woman, her sandy hair cut short but visible under her flat-crowned gray hat, standing there holding a Crow arrow in her hand. She wore a light denim jacket over a red-and-black-plaid shirt tucked into faded denim trousers.

"Dave," she said. "I'm so glad you're here. They killed my sheep."

"Hello, Evelyn," Jenner said. "Come on in."

She thrust the arrow at him and Jenner took it.

"Slocum, this is Evelyn Stark. Evelyn, do you know John Slocum?"

"No," she said, "I haven't had the pleasure. How do you do, Mr. Slocum."

Slocum stood up and offered her his hand. She shook it.

Her grip was strong and he saw working hands, with visible veins coursing beneath sun-tanned wrinkles.

"Pleased to meet you, ma'am," Slocum said.

Jenner examined the arrow, handed it to Slocum.

"Tell me what happened, Evelyn," he said.

"Some redskins with bows and arrows shot four of my sheep. They made off with three of them. I took this arrow out of another. Injuns. Can you imagine?"

"Crow," Slocum said.

"I don't know if they was Crow, Sioux, or Cheyenne," Evelyn said. "They was ridin' paints and wore quivers and had bows. They plumb kilt three of my sheep. The other one is crippled and I'll probably have to butcher it come morning."

"There are some renegade Crows in the mountains," Jenner said. "Slocum and I are going to go after them."

"I want payment for my sheep," she demanded.

"I doubt if you'll get any money from the Crow, but we'll sure try and see that they pay for sheep stealing and murder."

"Murder?"

"Didn't you hear about the stage robbery?" Jenner asked.

"Hell no. I been tendin' my flock."

Jenner told her about the ambush and the deaths. She cringed when she heard the names of the dead women.

"I guess my troubles are small compared to what happened to them poor women," she said. "Well, you can keep the arrow. Let me know if you catch them renegade redskins."

"I sure will, Evelyn. You better keep an eye out in case some of those Crow get hungry for mutton again. I hope we catch 'em before that happens."

"Good night, Dave. I swan, what's this world comin' to? I thought all the Injuns was on reservations."

She left and Slocum handed the arrow to Jenner. It did not have a flint arrowhead, but one made of thin tin sharpened to a surgical edge. The blade was covered with dried blood.

"I wonder where the Crow got these arrows," Slocum said. "I doubt if they made them on the reservation."

Jenner examined the arrow, sliding his finger up the shaft and touching the feathered fletching.

"These were made in Billings," he said. "Wood lathe, manufacture glue, dyed turkey feathers. The markings were added later. Someone sold or bought these arrows for the Crow."

"I agree," Slocum said. "Probably Valenti."

"Mmm. Could be. He said something today that might clear up that matter. But look, it's getting late. I'll buy you supper at the hotel and tell you what I overheard at that outlaw camp. We can talk to the Lorraines about going into hiding while we're there."

"You mean you'll talk to them," Slocum said.

"I mean, we'll both talk to them, John. You know 'em better'n I do."

"I don't know them at all. I just happened to find them up that logging road."

"They probably trust you, then. Come on, let's walk to the hotel. I'm starving. And I want to tell you more about what I overheard when Valenti and Pettibone were talking today."

"I'm all ears," Slocum said.

Jenner blew out the lamp. The two men left the darkened office. Jenner locked the door behind him. They walked down the street to the hotel with its windows glowing yellow and the night descending like a dark shroud over the street. The air was crisp and cool, and the sky filled with billions of dazzling stars.

There were people lounging in the lobby. Some waved to Jenner, who rushed past those entering the dining salon.

"Let's get a drink before we try and get a table," Jenner said. "Maybe the saloon's not so crowded."

"Who are all these people?" Slocum asked.

"I guess the Lorraines are a big hit, John."

They entered the saloon. All of the tables were taken, but there were stools at the bar. The two men sat down and Jenner ordered a whiskey and soda for himself.

"What'll you have, John?" he asked.

"Kentucky bourbon."

While they waited for the barkeep to pour their drinks, Slocum looked around the room. Most of the patrons were men, but he saw two women in fine clothes at one of the tables. Big Timber, he decided, was democratic, at least. Refined women did not usually frequent saloons. But, he supposed, since this one was in a hotel, it was really part of both the lobby and the dining salon.

The bartender set their drinks on the bartop and Jenner handed over some crumpled bills.

"Keep the change," he said. Then he turned to Slocum and raised his glass. "Luck," he said.

"Luck?"

"We're going to need some, I fear. Valenti strikes me as pretty smart."

"In what way?" Slocum asked.

"Well, when Pettibone brought up the matter of the Crow wanting white men's weapons, Valenti said he would not give them rifles, especially repeating rifles. When Pettibone asked why, Valenti said that as long as he and his bunch had rifles, the Crow would take orders. If he gave them rifles, they might turn on them."

"Sounds like Valenti's not sure of the Crow."

"He's got them under his thumb. For now."

"What else did you hear, Dave?"

"Valenti's got something planned, but he wouldn't tell Pettibone or any of the others I saw there. They were all griping about living up in those log cabins and wanting soft beds and loose women."

"Any hint of what Valenti's going to do?"

"One man, Macgregor, griped about Valenti's ex-wife, saying that it didn't get them any rewards."

"What did Valenti say to that?"

"He said the women were part of the deal and he would see to it that their pockets were filled with cash."

"Do you know what he meant by that?" Slocum asked.

Jenner shook his head.

"No town, no plan, was mentioned. Valenti keeps his cards close to his vest."

They finished their drinks and walked to the dining salon. There were few tables left, but the head waiter showed them to a table that was far from the stage. The small stage was lit up with lamps, but the candles for the footlights had not been lit. On stage were two guitars on wooden stands and a large poster announcing that night's performance by the Lorraines.

"Looks like Jasmine and her daughter will have a full house tonight," Jenner said.

"Are you going to them before or after they sing?" Slocum asked.

"Afterwards. Why ruin their evening and ours?"

A waiter took their order after he handed them one slate between them.

"Pork chops," Jenner said.

"Beef stew for me," Slocum said.

"Tomorrow we will have elk meat on the menu," the waiter said.

"Well cured, I hope," Slocum said, a sly curl to his lips.

"Oh yes," the waiter lied.

Jenner laughed.

"Nothing wrong with fresh elk meat, John."

"Nope. There were times when I would have eaten raw elk. I have eaten raw deer meat and a lizard or two."

"You must live an interesting life," Jenner said.

"If by interesting, you mean hard, yes."

"Seems to suit you."

"It interests me," Slocum said.

There was a hush in the dining room and several heads turned toward the entrance.

Slocum turned his head to see what caused the room to go so quiet.

Jasmine and Lydia, both dressed in pastel organdy gowns, blue for Jasmine and yellow for Lydia, entered the dining salon. They were trailed by Fenster, who preened and strutted like a gamecock. He waved to the patrons and stopped to speak at a table. The women walked slowly down the center aisle, then veered off in Slocum and Jenner's direction.

"Looks like they're headin' our way," Jenner said.

Slocum removed his hat and set it on an empty chair. When it seemed that the women were coming to his table, he stood up.

"John," Jasmine said, "I heard you were here. I'm so glad to see you."

"Me, too," Lydia said.

"Won't you sit down?" Jenner said as he rose from his chair.

"No thanks," Jasmine said. "We want to tune up and start the evening's entertainment. I just wanted to thank you both for coming."

"Our pleasure," Slocum said.

Jenner appeared to be suddenly tongue-tied.

"See you after the concert?" Jasmine said to Slocum.

"Why, sure, Jasmine. Matter of fact, Dave and I came to see you and wanted to talk with you after your performance."

"How very nice of you," Jasmine said.

Lydia's eyes brightened when she looked up at Slocum. He towered above her so that she looked smaller than she was.

"I hope you like our singing," Lydia said.

"I'm sure we will, Lydia." Slocum smiled at her and her eyes twinkled with pleasure.

"Until later, then," Jasmine said.

They walked to the stage amid whispers and admiring looks from the patrons. Soon, all the tables filled, and Slocum saw Fenster take a seat at a table near the stage.

"Fenster must be their chaperone," Jenner said as he sat down.

"A paid chaperone," Slocum said.

The women tuned their guitars. The audience fell silent.

Then they began to play, softly at first, then more loudly.

Jasmine began to sing and was joined in harmony by Lydia.

They looked like two angels, Slocum thought, and their voices blended perfectly, sweetly, as they sang "Dixie," then changed to the "Battle Hymn of the Republic." The audience cheered and the women smiled and segued into another tune, "Jeanie with the Light Brown Hair."

The audience erupted in a thunderous round of applause when the women finished and bowed.

"It would be easy to fall in love with them women," Jenner said. "Just watchin' them sing."

"Yes," Slocum murmured. He was deep in thought.

It was hard to imagine that there was a man out there who wanted to cause them harm, who wanted what he could not have, Jasmine. Valenti, he thought, must have a heart of iron, not to mention a diabolic soul.

Yes, he thought, he could fall in love with either woman. Or both.

16

Slocum and Jenner were among the last to finish their suppers. Waiters cleared the tables and many of the patrons ordered cordials and aperitifs as after-dinner drinks. Jasmine and Lydia had the audience enthralled. They sang "Greensleeves" and other folk songs to thunderous applause at the end of each number.

Just then, another sound burst over the applause. The crowd stopped their clapping and went silent. Slocum stood up. Jenner stared at him, a look of surprise on his face.

"What's that?" Jenner said.

"Gunshots," Slocum said.

Two more gunshots rattled the windows in the room and people slid from their chairs to crawl under the tables.

Slocum started toward the lobby, his right hand gripping the butt of his revolver.

A moment later, a man screamed.

"Help me, help me!" he shouted.

The voice came from the hotel lobby.

Jenner rose from his chair and ran after Slocum.

Slocum saw a man stagger into the lobby. His left arm dripped blood.

"He's still out there," the man said, and collapsed to the floor.

Slocum drew his pistol and rushed outside. He bent over in a crouch as he hurried down the front steps. He saw two horses in the middle of the street. Nearby, there was the figure of a man.

Just as Slocum cleared the last step, another shot cracked the night with a stream of orange flame. Slocum ducked down as a bullet plowed a furrow inches from the step. He cocked his pistol and pulled the trigger, firing at the afterimage of the glowing spume of flame.

He heard footsteps on the boardwalk across the street. Fifty yards away, he saw another horse standing hipshot under a streetlamp. Slocum recognized the horse, a buckskin with cropped mane and tale, part Arab and part Morgan.

It was one of the horses he had sold to Bruno Valenti in Billings.

The man lying on the street groaned in pain. Across the street, Slocum saw a large man duck into a space between two buildings. He fired another shot, then heard the sound of retreating footsteps.

"I'm bad hurt," the man on the ground moaned.

Slocum, still in a crouch, went to him.

"Who shot you?" he asked.

"I don't know. We been chased for miles. I think I'm bleeding to death."

"You hold on," Slocum said.

He saw blood pouring from a hole in the man's side, and another from his leg.

Jenner came down the steps, his pistol drawn.

"Dave, can you help this man? I know where the shooter went. And keep your eye on that buckskin down the street. It's under that streetlamp."

Jenner looked over and saw the buckskin horse.

Slocum stood up.

"The man inside is shot, too," he told Slocum. "He and two other men were hunting a cougar and stumbled onto Valenti's camp. Valenti killed one man up there and then someone chased these two back here to Big Timber."

"This man needs a doctor, Dave."

Slocum ran off to the corner of the block, bent on finding the man who had shot at him. He heard Jenner talking to some people who had come out of the hotel.

He passed the buckskin and turned the corner at the end of the block. He stopped and listened, flattening himself against the frame of a wooden building that housed a fishing tackle store. While he waited, he ejected the hulls of the two bullets he had fired, pulled fresh cartridges from their belt loops, and thumbed them into the empty chambers of the cylinder. He spun the cylinder and pulled the hammer back to half-cock. Then he crept along the building to the next street over, stopping every few steps to listen.

He heard the crunch of a boot on the next street as he reached the corner. There, he leaned against cold bricks and waited.

Someone was walking his way. And the person was very careful. One step, then another. Stop, and then another step.

Crunch, crunch.

Slocum ducked down and craned his neck to see around the corner.

The street was not lighted. It was dark and filled with thick shadows, some bulging, some thin and rectangular, some triangular or trapezoid-shaped.

One of the shadows moved. There were no boardwalks in front of the stores with their dim false fronts or obscure glass windows. As the shadow moved, it made another crunching noise. The shadow moved toward him, one step at a time. In the dim light of the stars and the streetlamp on Main Street, Slocum saw the gleam of a pistol, just a brief and momentary glint of light as the man moved his hand when he took another cautious step.

Slocum measured the distance in his mind, estimated the yardage between him and the approaching man.

No more than thirty yards, he figured.

Still too far for a certain shot.

He knew that combinations of light, low light, and darkness, played tricks on a man's eyesight. If he fired his pistol now, he might shoot high or low. Or he might be off to one side or the other. Better to wait.

The man was probably trying to sneak back to the other street and climb onto his horse. He had no other place to go, and few ways to get there.

So Slocum waited. He pulled his head back and stood up straight. He gently squeezed the trigger and hammered back to full cock.

He slowed his breathing, listened for another footfall.

Crunch. Crunch.

He could hear barely discernible voices coming from the street in front of the hotel.

Crunch, crunch.

Voices fading and rising, fading again. Muffled voices. Distant chatter. Low tones.

Then, no more voices.

Just a long silence.

Again, the crunch of a boot on sand and gravel.

How much closer? Slocum wondered.

Time ticked away in Slocum's mind. Like a clock. A pendulum swaying. A faint tick, tick, tick.

The waiting became a heavy weight on Slocum's shoulder, a weight that ticked and drew sweat from his pores.

Close and closer the man came, his footsteps growing ever louder. The crunches seemed to be so close that Slocum had to restrain himself from leaping out of hiding and blasting away at the ghostly presence only a few yards away.

Still he waited. He held his breath.

Another crunch, and then another.

The last one sounded so close, Slocum felt as if the man would appear at any second. He thought the man might round the corner and stand inches away, that pistol of his bury itself in Slocum's gut.

He let out his breath slow.

Then he drew another and held it.

No matter what happened next, Slocum knew that he had the advantage. However, if he made one mistake, the man would blow a hole in him and he might well die while the gunman ran off and retrieved his horse.

Still, he waited, telling himself he would spring out of hiding and start shooting in the next ten seconds or so.

Crunch, scrape, crunch.

Now Slocum could hear the man's heavy breathing. He heard it or he imagined it. He couldn't be sure.

The man was close. The next step was a loud crunch of boot.

Slocum could wait no longer.

He went into a fighting crouch and slid his body around the corner of the brick building.

"Drop it," he said.

The shadowy man was less than five yards away when Slocum thumbed the hammer back to full cock. The man's arm moved as he raised his pistol to fire at Slocum.

The ticking in Slocum's head stopped.

He squeezed the trigger and the Colt barked, bucked against the palm of his hand. Orange and blue flame burst from the barrel like a comet with trailing sparks. The man grunted as the lead bullet smacked into his belly. He jerked and Slocum fired again, raising the barrel slightly higher. The man was close enough to see plainly and there was no distortion because of low light or darkness.

The slug caught the man square in the chest and Slocum

saw a dark stem spew into a black flower in the man's chest. He sagged to his knees and gasped for a breath that was not there; that would never be there again.

The man's gun spun downward, its barrel pointing at the street. He slumped to his knees and tried to lift his head. He toppled forward onto his face. His fingers went slack and the unfired pistol fell from his grasp.

The echoes from the two shots faded away among the buildings and the distant trees.

Slocum stood up straight and drew in a long heavy breath.

The night was chill and the breath felt good in his chest.

He slid his pistol back in his holster and walked over to the man. He toed him with his boot. The man's body lifted and half-turned, then slumped back to where it had been.

Slocum knew the man was dead.

He turned him over and looked at his face. Even in the dark, he knew it was a face he had never seen before.

He grabbed the man by his collar and dragged him around the building and down to Main Street. He left him by the buckskin, and walked to the hotel. The horse would not go anywhere. Slocum knew the animal, had brought him to Montana all the way from Missouri. The buckskin wasn't gun-shy and he wasn't a runaway that spooked at every shadow or noise.

There was a splotch of blood where the wounded man had lain.

Slocum looked at it and let out a sigh.

He braced himself for what he might find when he went back inside the hotel.

This had been a deadly night and he knew there were stories yet to be heard. Hunters, men tracking a cougar, had ventured into Valenti's outlaw camp and found themselves in a hornet's nest.

The horses they had ridden in were flecked with dried foam, sweat. The buckskin, as well, had those same streaks on its light tan hide. The horses had been ridden hard, out of fear, and the lone gunman sent to silence them had almost done it.

Almost.

Slocum looked up at the night sky.

As usual, the stars were impervious to what happened on this small planet so far away from their brilliance.

Like the mountains, they were eternal and wise, and darkness was their domain.

17

Slocum stepped onto the hotel porch. He could see people milling around in the lobby. One of them, Donnie, burst through the front door with its cut glass inlay and rushed up to the hatless man.

"Mr. Slocum, where you been? Two of our guests have been shot. They're inside."

"I know, Donnie. Look, I need you to do something for me."

"Sure, anything, Mr. Slocum."

"First, tie up these loose horses in front of the hotel. Go get that buckskin down the street and bring it back here and secure it."

"Sure, Mr. Slocum."

"There's one other thing, son. Go back down to the end of the block where the buckskin is, and go to that next street yonder. You'll find a six-gun lying in the dirt. Bring it back to me and be damned careful. It's loaded."

"Okay." Donnie seemed ready to leap from the porch. Slocum put his hand flat on Donnie's chest to keep him from running off to accomplish those tasks.

113

"There's a dead man near that buckskin. Don't look at him or touch him."

"A dead man?"

"An outlaw I just shot," Slocum said.

"Holy cow. You shot an outlaw?"

"Get going," Slocum said, and pulled his hand back. Donnie dashed down the steps and ran to one of the hunters' horses.

Slocum walked into the hotel lobby with its overstuffed chairs and divans, its potted plants and gawking spectators, all staring down at the two wounded men. Jenner kneeled next to one of them. He was trying to staunch the bleeding with towels. Ray Mallory stood over him, holding a stack of washcloths.

Jasmine and Lydia were among the onlookers. Their faces were drawn, but with their ruffled bodices, they looked like two flowers among a plot of weeds. Fenster stood there, rigid as a post. His face was impassive and expressionless. In his drab suit, he looked like a mourner at a pauper's funeral.

Both women looked at Slocum, their eyes wide and bright.

"Ray," Slocum said to Mallory, "can you get all these people out of the lobby and back into the dining room?"

Mallory appeared stunned and bewildered. But he snapped out of it and spoke to the people around him.

"Please, folks," he said, "return to the dining salon. Jasmine, will you and your daughter please return to the stage?"

Jasmine nodded, and with one last glance at Slocum, she and her daughter led the procession back down the hall to the dining room.

"Thanks, John," Jenner said. He glanced up at Slocum, a look of helplessness on his face.

Soon, only Jenner, Mallory, the desk clerk, and Slocum remained in the lobby. Slocum looked at the first man he had seen rushing into the lobby, yelling for help. He sat on the floor in a dazed state, his face contorted in pain. His trousers were wet with blood and he was putting pressure on the wound in his leg.

"Did you get him?" the man said to Slocum.

"John, this is Luther Bradley, one of the hunters staying here at the hotel."

"Was there just one man chasing you?" Slocum asked.

"Far as I know. Me and Lou Tinsley there barely escaped with our lives. We near run our horses to death gettin' here. Them sonsabitches killed our friend Jasper Langley. Shot him right in the head before we knew what we'd run into."

"I got the man who chased you," Slocum said.

"He's dead?" Bradley said.

"As a doornail," Slocum replied.

Bradley looked over at his wounded friend.

"Is Lou going to make it?" he asked Jenner.

Jenner shook his head. "He's shot up pretty bad. Lost too much blood."

"For Christ's sake, Ray, don't you have a doctor in this damned town?" Bradley gave Mallory an accusing look.

"We got one, Luther, but he might be out to one of the ranches. I sent for him."

"This man's beyond doctoring," Jenner said, and sat down on his haunches, his arms limp at his sides. They all heard the dying man's breath as he fought for his life. Soon, Tinsley began to wheeze and his chest rose and fell like a bellows as his breathing became more difficult.

It was painful to watch, Slocum thought. His jaw hardened as he watched Tinsley in the last throes of dying. Tinsley's eyes fluttered open and closed, and each time he opened them, they became glassier and more cloudy.

There was a slight gurgle that sounded like pebbles rattling in an air-tight jar. His body twitched a few times and then was still.

"We lost him, looks like," Mallory said.

Jenner put two fingers beneath Tinsley's chin, pressing

on the carotid artery. He left them there for several seconds, then sighed and took his hand away.

"Yeah, he's gone," Jenner said.

He stood up, walked over to Slocum.

"You say you shot one of 'em?" he asked.

"I think there was only one."

"I better take a look," Jenner said.

"He's outside, in the street. Follow me," Slocum said.

Jenner turned to Mallory.

"Coroner ought to be here any minute. Have him take Tinsley to the morgue."

"I will," Mallory said. He helped Bradley to his feet. "I'll take you to your room," he said. "I'll have the doc look in on you as soon as he shows up. Maybe tomorrow."

"I can make it until then. If I don't bleed no more."

Slocum and Jenner walked out of the hotel. They met Donnie outside. He was wrapping the buckskin's reins around a hitchrail. He drew a pistol from his belt and handed it to Slocum.

"Here's that pistol you told me to get, Mr. Slocum."

"Thanks, Donnie. See if your pa needs any help. There's another dead man in the lobby."

"Another one? God amighty. What a night."

Donnie took the steps two at a time and disappeared on the other side of the hotel's double doors.

"What did you find out, Dave?" Slocum asked as the two men walked toward the streetlamp and the still figure lying in the street, just beyond the pale circle of tawny light.

"Seems like three men were tracking a cougar up near that old loggers' camp. They rode in and were attacked by Valenti and his men. Valenti killed one man outright. The two in there lit a shuck, and knew they were being chased. They got to town and the shooting started. You know the rest pretty much."

"Now Valenti will know that we know where he is."

"Yeah, he'll probably figure it out. He may move his

camp, or show up here. We've still got to talk to Jasmine and Lydia, get them someplace safe."

Jenner kneeled down to look at the man Slocum had shot.

He turned the dead man's face toward the streetlight, examined it closely.

"That's one of 'em, all right," he said. "Man's name is Angus Macgregor. There's a two-hundred-dollar bounty on him. Dead or alive. It looks like you made yourself a little money, John."

"The hard way," Slocum said. "And I sold Valenti that buckskin Macgregor was riding."

"Then it looks like you've got yourself a horse and saddle, a rifle, six-gun, belt, and holster."

"To the victor belongs the spoils, Dave?"

"Absolutely."

Jenner stood up.

"Looks like the coroner's going to be busy again."

"Not to mention the undertaker," Slocum said.

The two men walked slowly back to the hotel.

They could hear the Lorraines singing as they approached.

Their voices quavered in the clear night air, harmonizing on "Camptown Races."

"They won't want to leave," Slocum said.

"They've got to leave. Once Valenti finds out that Macgregor's not coming back, he'll figure two men know about his hideout. He'll make a move."

"He won't know right away."

"That gives us some time," Jenner said. "And my little posse will be at my office at sunup."

"You going up there after Valenti?"

"That's all I can do," Jenner said.

"You'll be outnumbered with only you and three men."

"Four men, counting you, John."

Slocum halted at the hitchrail.

"I haven't been deputized," he said.

"I'll do that first thing in the morning."

"Maybe we ought to spend the rest of the night making out our wills," Slocum said.

"If you make out yours, put me down as your beneficiary, will you? Because I aim to get out of this alive."

"You wouldn't get much. A couple of horses, some tack, guns and ammunition, a few measly dollars."

"Well, that's more'n I came into this world with, John."

"Sunup, eh?"

"Sunup," Jenner said.

"It looks like tomorrow's going to be another long day," Slocum said.

"And this one ain't over yet," Jenner said. "We still have to have a little talk with them gals."

"What about Fenster? He'll have something to say about those women leaving town."

"I'll take care of Fenster," Jenner said.

"How?"

Jenner grinned.

"I'll lock him up as a material witness if he gives us a hard time."

"You've been too long at the law books, Dave."

"Just enough."

As the two men ascended the steps, they heard the Lorraines break into another lively number. They were singing "Little Brown Jug."

"Not a bad idea," Slocum said.

"I could use a taste myself."

The two walked back into the hotel. Someone had put a blanket over the dead man. There was no one at the desk, nor in the lobby.

The two men went straight to the saloon. The room was packed, but they could hear the music from there.

And they could hear the riotous applause for the Lorraines.

"Memory is a funny thing," Slocum said as they sidled up to the bar.

"Oh? How so?"

"It doesn't last long. You hear a song or two and the dead are forgotten."

"Ain't that why they sing hymns at funerals, John?"

"I reckon. Music hath charms to soothe the savage breast."

"I thought it was 'beast.'"

Slocum looked at Jenner with a hard stare.

"You ever sing to a charging bull or a bear? It's 'breast.'"

"I stand corrected," Jenner said.

As they drank, Jenner and Slocum listened to the Lorraines singing an old-time hymn with poignancy and feeling.

The song was "Bringing In the Sheaves."

"Makes a man want to cry, don't it, Slocum?"

Slocum said nothing. He was remembering his boyhood in Georgia when he had to go to church with his mam and pap.

All the singing in the world won't bring back the dead, he thought.

The bourbon warmed his throat and his belly. The pistol in his belt was starting to chafe. A dead man's pistol, and a Colt to boot.

Life did have its rewards, he thought. And death had none.

18

Jenner left the dining salon when Mallory notified him of the coroner's arrival, but Slocum stayed to listen to the Lorraines.

Jasmine looked at him often during the remainder of the concert. Lydia seemed unaware of her mother's attention to Slocum. The audience rose to its feet when they finished their final number and took their bows. The patrons were slow to leave, but Jasmine walked to Slocum's table and sat down while Lydia finished tidying up the stage.

"I'm so glad you were able to see Lydia and me perform, John," she said.

"It was a pleasure."

"I wonder if you'd consider coming up to our room for a libation."

"If a libation means a drink, I'd like that," he said.

Jasmine laughed, and her laugh was as beautiful and as sonorous as her voice.

"I know you favor Kentucky bourbon and it so happens I have a bottle up in the room."

"I'm surprised. Kentucky bourbon's hard to get out here in the hinterlands."

"The hinterlands. Is that where we are?"

They both laughed.

"Fenster was able to obtain a bottle from the hotel," she said.

"Will Mr. Fenster be joining us?" Slocum asked.

"No, he surely will not. And neither will my daughter. Mr. Fenster has invited her to his room."

"Oh?"

"It's not what you think, John. Lydia is also my business manager as well as my bookkeeper. She and Fenster must go over the new contracts Mr. Mallory has given us and settle accounts to date."

"I think Dave Jenner would like to be invited up for a drink also," Slocum said.

Jasmine hesitated, then recovered quickly.

"I thought he was off chasing those bad men who attacked us," she said. "But of course, he can come. I have whiskey and cordials, too."

Slocum puffed on his cheroot. Through the haze of blue smoke he saw Lydia pick up a large bowl that was at the corner of the stage. The bowl was filled with paper currency, bills put there by the appreciative patrons. Fenster walked up to the stage and spoke to Lydia. He couldn't hear what Fenster said, but he saw Lydia swing the bowl to her side and then put it behind her.

Fenster stepped up to the stage and reached out for Lydia. She retreated, but Fenster pursued her. He ran to her side and grabbed one edge of the bowl. He pulled on it and Lydia pulled back. For that instant, the two were locked in mortal combat over the contents of the fishbowl.

"Excuse me, Jasmine," Slocum said. He rose from his chair. His eyes were narrowed and he was staring at Fenster and Lydia, who were still engaged in a tug-of-war over the glass bowl.

"Where are you going?" she asked as Slocum swept by her, the cheroot in his mouth trailing smoke past his face as if from a locomotive.

"Your daughter's having a tussle with Fenster," he said.

Jasmine whirled around and looked at the stage. Slocum was halfway there when she bolted from her chair and started to run after him.

Slocum got there first and climbed onto the stage. He grabbed Fenster by his suit collar and jerked him backward. Lydia held on to the bowl and almost fell as she backpedaled, suddenly released from the opposing energy exerted by Fenster.

"Leave her alone, Fenster," Slocum said. He looked down at the man, whose face was contorted in rage.

"You stay out of this, Slocum," Fenster snarled.

"What's going on here, Lydia?" he asked. She gripped the bowl in her arms as if daring anyone to wrest it from her grasp.

Jasmine bounded on to the stage, her dress fanning the candle flames that served as footlights. She glared at Fenster, who tried to shrug out of Slocum's grasp.

"Leroy's trying to take our tip money," Lydia said.

"I deserve my cut," Fenster said, a bitter bite to his words.

"That's our money," Jasmine said. "You have no right to any of it, Leroy."

"Read your contract, Jasmine. I get a percentage of all the money you and Lydia take in."

"Not our tip money," Lydia wailed, her voice rising to a hysterical pitch.

"That's right," Jasmine said.

Fenster tried to pull away from Slocum, but Slocum pulled him backward by the collar.

"Let go of me," Fenster said.

"I'll let go of you when you begin to act like a gentleman," Slocum said.

"You've got no right," Fenster growled. His lips curled

in a feral snarl as he glared up at Slocum, his eyes filled with the fires of rage.

"I'm taking the right, Fenster," Slocum said. "That money in the bowl is the audience's way of showing their appreciation for these ladies. It was meant for them, not for you."

Slocum reached into his pants pocket and pulled out a five-dollar note. He held it out to Lydia.

"Here," he said. "This is for you and your mother. I enjoyed your fine singing."

Lydia smiled and reached out for the bill.

Jasmine looked up at Slocum, an expression of gratitude on her face.

Fenster fumed, but he could go nowhere, and Lydia still embraced the bowl of money now graced with another greenback. His eyes rolled around in their sockets like a pair of ball bearings blackened by smoke. His face contorted into a shriveled mass of quivering flesh.

"All right, all right," Fenster spluttered. "You win this round, ladies, but—"

"No buts, Fenster," Slocum interrupted. "That tip money belongs to the performing ladies. Your commission comes from contracts you arrange for their performances. Two separate things."

"You ain't no lawyer, Slocum," Fenster spat.

"No, I'm not a lawyer, but you're only an employee of these women. They can fire you if they want to and all you'll have is a pile of blank paper you can take with you to the outhouse."

"Damn you, Slocum," Fenster said.

"If you cause any more trouble, I'll throw you off this stage, Fenster. Now, get the hell out of here and forget about that bowl of money."

"I—I . . ." Fenster sputtered, unable to retort.

"You'd better leave, Leroy," Jasmine said. "Lydia will be up in a while to look over those new contracts, won't you, Lydia?"

"I might," Lydia said.

"And when you two finish talking—reasonably, I hope— she'll bring the contracts to me. Tomorrow, or the next day, I'll let you know if we'll sign with you as our manager."

"You can't just dump me, Jasmine," Fenster said. "I got you where you are. I'm building your names. I'm your only hope of success."

"Oh, I don't know about that, Leroy," Jasmine said. "A man from Bozeman owns saloons all over Montana and spoke to me about playing in Great Falls, Helena, and Missoula."

"What? Who is he?"

Jasmine smiled.

"I don't think he would like you as our manager, Leroy. He said he could keep us working year-round, and there would be no middleman."

"I'd like to—"

"You've had your say, Fenster," Slocum said. "Now, get out or I'll throw you out. In the street."

Slocum released his hold on Fenster's collar. Fenster huffed and puffed, but he turned and bounded off the stage, stalking across the room like a little martinet.

"Ma, did you really speak to a man from Bozeman?" Lydia asked.

"No, but I'm sure we will as news of our performances gets around."

Slocum looked at Jasmine with admiration.

She turned to Lydia.

"Take that bowl up to our room," she said. "Count it and hide it under the mattress. Then you talk to Leroy and tell him we'll only pay him five percent from now on."

"Really?" Lydia said, her face aglow.

"Really, darling. Now run along. John and I will join you shortly."

Lydia traipsed off the stage, holding the bowl as if it were a large golden egg. Jasmine watched her go.

"You have a lot of spunk," Slocum said to her.

"So does Lydia," she said. "Shall we go upstairs or have a drink in the saloon?"

"Jenner and I need to talk to you, Jasmine. It would be more private in your room."

"Or yours," she said softly, sidling next to him and slipping her arm inside his. "I don't really need a drink tonight. I just want to kick off my high-heeled shoes and relax."

"My room is pretty bare, but I do have a bottle of good bourbon."

"I could develop a taste for bourbon."

"I warn you," he said, "it's fatal. You won't want to drink anything else for the rest of your life."

"I could live with that, I think."

He patted the back of her hand.

"My room it is," he said. "We'll let Dave Jenner know."

They walked, arm in arm, through the nearly empty room. One of the waiters went to the stage carrying a long brass rod with a hollow bell on one end. He snuffed out all the candles, and the stage went dark.

Jasmine looked back when she reached the hallway.

"It looks so sad," she said. "That empty stage. Tugs at my heart."

"You brought life to it," he said. "You and Lydia."

"Yes, we did, didn't we?"

The coroner, one Jove Abelard, and his minions were just going out the front door of the hotel, Tinsley's shrouded body on a stretcher. Jenner watched them go then turned to find Slocum and Jasmine emerging from the hallway. The lobby was empty, and there was nobody at the desk.

"Dave," Slocum said, "we're going up to my room for a drink. All I have is bourbon."

Jenner smiled.

"That's good enough for me. Did you talk to Miss Lorraine yet?"

"Not yet."

"What about?" Jasmine asked.

"It can wait," Slocum said, and whirled her to the stairs. Jenner trailed behind them.

She touched the butt of the outlaw's gun sticking out of Slocum's belt as they ascended the stairs.

"Do you need so many guns?" she whispered, a trace of mirth in her voice.

"A souvenir," he said.

"I'll bet you have another gun or two hidden away somewhere on your person," she said. Slocum detected a decidedly teasing tone in her voice.

"One or two," he said.

He did have a hideout gun, what some people called a Remington belly gun. That one was his ace in the hole.

"I'd like to see all your guns sometime," she said, and there was a husk to her voice that brought a flush of crimson to his face.

"I didn't think guns interested the ladies much," he said.

"Some guns do," she said, and pinched him on the waist.

The walk down the hallway to his room seemed to take forever. Jasmine clung to him like a girl at her first school dance with her beau.

He was sorry that Jenner was right behind them.

But, he thought, he would see to it that the sheriff did not stay long. After all, they both had an early start in the morning.

Slocum opened the door to his room.

"Wait here until I light the lamp," he told Jasmine. He walked into the dark room and fumbled with the matches and lamp. Finally, the wick caught flame and light spilled into the modest room.

"Welcome," he said to Jasmine as she entered through the door.

Jenner followed and went straight to the highboy, where

the liquor bottle was gleaming in the lamplight. There were extra glasses, as Mallory had promised. Jenner poured himself a drink.

"Anyone else?" he said.

"I'll pour ours," Slocum said, with the emphasis on the last word so that Dave could catch his drift. "Set yourself down, Dave."

Jasmine went to the small divan and sat down. She looked like a garden in bloom, with her patent leather high-heeled shoes, her slender legs, and the organdy dress with the ruffled bodice.

Slocum thought she looked perfectly at home. He thought she would look at home and comfortable anywhere she happened to be. She was beautiful. She was lovely. And, he was sure, she wanted him as much as he wanted her.

19

Jenner sat down in a chair at the table. He faced Jasmine on the divan. Slocum drew Macgregor's pistol from his belt and put it in a bureau drawer, unbuckled his gun belt and hung it on a chair, then walked to the bar, turning to speak to Jasmine.

"Two fingers or four?" he asked.

"One finger," she said. "One dainty little finger."

Slocum laughed and poured bourbon into two glasses.

"Water?" he asked.

"Yes, please."

He poured water in another glass and carried her drink and the glass to her, set it on the small table in front of the divan. He walked back and got his own drink, two fingers of clear amber liquid. He sat down next to her on the divan, raised his glass to her.

"To a fine performance," he said.

"Thank you." She took a small sip of her drink. Slocum watched her. She sloshed the bourbon around in her mouth and swallowed, then gasped for breath.

"My," she said, "that is a bit stout."

Jenner and Slocum both laughed and swallowed mouthfuls of bourbon.

"Jasmine," Jenner said as he leaned toward her in his chair, "I can't stay long. Slocum and I are going after Bruno and his gang early in the morning."

"You are?" she said, with a sidelong glance at Slocum.

"Yes, and I have a request to make of you," Jenner said.

"Oh?"

"Yes. I, we, that is, John and I think you and your daughter are in great danger. I overheard Bruno talking to one of his men about coming here to kidnap you and Miss Lydia."

"That doesn't surprise me," she said. "Bruno is a vicious man and he can't get over his anger about my divorcing him."

"He's a very dangerous man, as you well know. He's already killed several people and may have raped those two old women."

"Bruno a rapist?" Jasmine shook her head. "No, Bruno has trouble with women. He had a problem with me. He—well, I won't go into it here, but in his mind, all women are evil, and when it comes to, well, you know, he's a failure."

Jenner sat up straight. Her words caught him by surprise. Slocum, too, seemed taken aback, but he showed no sign that he was either shocked or surprised by what Jasmine had said.

"Don't look so shocked, Sheriff," she said. "There are men like that. I think they secretly hate women, or more likely, they're scared of them. I think Bruno was intimidated by his mother. He said he hated her, but he stayed with her until well after he had reached the age of manhood."

"I wouldn't know," Jenner said. "I mean, I don't know any man like that."

"Consider yourself lucky," Jasmine said.

"That doesn't negate the fact that Bruno wants to kidnap

you and your daughter. Maybe he hates you both and means to do you harm."

"Oh, he hates us both, I'm sure," Jasmine said. "And as for hurting us, he already has."

"He might murder you both," Jenner said, his voice icy hot, his brows knotted up like dark ropes.

"Can't you protect me, Sheriff? You said you were going after him tomorrow."

"The man's a loose cannon on a pitching deck," Jenner said. Slocum sipped his drink, watching Jenner squirm to get his message across. "I'd like to take you and your daughter out of town until we catch Bruno Valenti. For a few days. Please. I have a hunting cabin up in Paradise Valley, near Livingston. You and Miss Lydia would be perfectly safe there."

"I'm sure we would," Jasmine said. "Perfectly safe, and bored, and lonesome, unable to do what we love to do, sing for the public."

"If I took you there, you'd live to sing your hearts out," Jenner said.

"It's out of the question, Sheriff. Lydia and I are doing well here in Big Timber. Mr. Mallory wants us to stay on, for at least a month, maybe longer. I feel that when Leroy gets the word out about us, we'll pack the dining salon. Our salaries will go up and we can perform in other towns, like Livingston, and Bozeman, maybe Helena and Missoula."

"That may be so," Jenner said, "but I'm urging you to let me take you to a safe place for at least a day or two. You can come back to the hotel and continue to sing."

"Do I have a choice?" Jasmine said. She looked at Slocum, whose face was a noncommittal mask. He did not move, but just sat there, quiet and impassive, as if he had willed himself to be somewhere else, away from this room and the conversation.

"Well, yeah," Jenner said. "I can't force you to do what I

ask. But I'm begging you, for your own safety. John here agrees with me, don't you, John?"

Slocum was forced to return to the room and become part of the conversation.

"Yes, Dave, I think Jasmine and Lydia might be in danger. However, they also have their careers to think about. If they left now, at the moment of what could be a triumph for them, they could sink like stones in a dark sea. The people who were there tonight might think they were too uppity, and had abandoned them."

"Oh, John, that's so much horseshit and you know it," Jenner said, his anger rising, his neck reddening like the line in a thermometer.

"Could you guarantee their safety in, where is it, Paradise Valley?" Slocum asked. "I mean, they'd be in your hunting cabin all by themselves, with no one to watch over them. Two beautiful women, all alone. There are probably other Brunos out there who would like to get their hands on them."

"John, you're making it hard for me," Jenner said. "You're siding with Miss Jasmine and leaving me without a leg to stand on."

"Well, Dave, you asked me."

"And now, I'm sorry I did." He turned to look at Jasmine. "One last time, Miss Jasmine. Will you let me take you and your daughter up to Paradise Valley tonight, where I know you'll be safe? I might even be able to bring you back tomorrow afternoon and you won't miss your performance."

Jasmine sighed.

She gave Jenner an open and honest look, her blue eyes unblinking.

"Lydia and I will be perfectly safe here, Sheriff. We do not want to go riding off in the middle of the night to some deserted place where wolves and bears and mountain lions prowl."

She lifted her skirt up to her knees and showed Jenner

and Slocum her stockinged leg. Just above her knee, there was a small holster. The butt of a Derringer showed above the leather.

"This gun has two bullets in it, Sheriff. And I know how to use it. I don't intend for Bruno to kidnap me or Lydia. If he tries, I'll shoot him dead."

She let her skirt drop and smoothed out her dress. Jenner's mouth was agape and his eyes were stuck wide open.

Slocum took another swallow of bourbon. Jasmine raised her glass to her lips and sipped a tiny bit, then set it back down.

Jenner finished his drink and slammed the glass down hard on the table.

"All right, Miss Jasmine," he said, "you win. I'll slink on out of here and forget I've been trying to save your life. I hope we get Bruno in the morning. But if not, don't say I didn't warn you. That man's as treacherous as a sidewinder and he could grab you and your daughter without you ever knowing he was there. And if he knows you have that peashooter strapped to your leg, he'll probably shoot you dead before you can lift your skirt."

Jenner stalked across the room without waiting for an answer. He stormed out of the room and slammed the door behind him.

Slocum heard his boots pound on the carpeted hall until the sound faded into silence.

"I think you hurt Dave's feelings," Slocum said as he turned to her.

She scooted closer to him on the divan.

"He's a worrywart," she said.

"He has your best interests at heart."

Jasmine snuggled up to him, put her head in the hollow just below his shoulder.

"You'll protect me, won't you, John? I mean, if Bruno were to burst through that door right now, you'd shoot him dead, wouldn't you?"

Her question, thought Slocum, did not require an answer. He could smell her perfume, the musk of her perspiration, the heady scent of her femaleness. If Bruno were to walk in on them at that moment, he doubted if he could retrieve his pistol fast enough to fire at him.

"You're not going to answer me, are you?" she said finally, after seconds had passed.

"I'd protect you if I was around when Bruno came after you. I may not be."

"He won't dare come here," she said. "And he doesn't know you, doesn't know what you look like."

"That's true. There's no assurance that we'll catch him tomorrow. From what Dave says, he's pretty smart."

"Oh, he's cunning, all right. Like a fox. But inside, he's a coward, like most men."

"You think most men are cowards?"

"Men I've known," she said.

"Then you probably never knew a soldier or a sheriff like Dave Jenner. He's no coward."

"No, I don't believe he is. And you certainly are not."

"How do you know that?" he asked.

"I know," she said. "I can judge men. I see enough of them to know what they want, and most don't have the courage to ask for it, or go after it without simpering and cowing down like beggars."

"So, you have us all figured out, do you?"

She did not answer.

Instead, she moved her body and threw her arms around his neck. She pushed her lips against his and crushed them.

Slocum felt the heat rise through his body like a prairie storm. Then her hand was in his crotch and squeezing him. He felt his member engorge with blood and harden into a shaft that threatened to bust his buttons.

"This is the gun I wanted to see," she whispered and kissed him again.

Slocum felt as if he were falling, falling into a garden of

flowers where the wine was hot and the moon glazed him with a silvery frost. It was the next thing to paradise, he thought, and took her in his arms and kissed her with all his might.

He felt her body soften against his.

"I'll blow out the lamp," he said huskily.

"Yes, do," she said.

He walked to the lamp in a half-daze, his mind racing like a windmill in a twister.

He heard Jasmine walk to the door and drop the bar that locked them in. Then there was the whisper of her clothes when she walked back to the bed.

When he saw her again, she was naked and as alluring as a siren. She began to undress him, and when she took off his boots, he slipped his trousers down and she could see for herself that he was ready, and that he was hers for the taking.

20

Slocum and Jasmine collapsed on the bed together, locked in each other's embrace. They rolled to the center, peppering each other's faces with kisses. He felt her hot breath on his face as she swarmed over him with her lips.

"Oh, John," she whispered in between kisses, "I want you, want you, so much."

He could not reply because her mouth was on his and her tongue was laving his own, swabbing and probing the recesses of his mouth.

Her hand grasped his stalk and squeezed. Then she pumped her hand up and down, making his organ swell into a throbbing mass of flesh as thick as a man's wrist.

He probed the warm velvet chamber of her sex, inserting a finger. He found the tiny bud that was her clitoris and plucked it with his fingertip. Her back arched and she convulsed with pleasure, her mouth sliding down to his neck. She sucked until the blood rushed to his skin and then her hand was on his chest, her fingers threading through the wiry tangle.

Her body bucked and thrashed as they wallowed atop the bed, each exploring with lips and hands, the crevices and valleys, the mounds and softnesses of their bodies. He gripped her buttocks and then her breasts. She slid her mouth down to his manhood and took his throbbing cock's head between her lips, tickling the eyelet with the tip of her tongue. Then she slid his prick inside her mouth and he felt the warmth of her saliva as she slid his member in and out. She breathed heavily and made animal noises. He grabbed a handful of her hair and pushed against her face, and she gagged as the tip of his cock struck the back of her throat.

She was ready. And so was he.

He flipped her over on her back. She spread her legs wide and cocked them slightly as he rose above her, his arms stiff, his loins lowering to hers.

"Now," she breathed. "Take me, John. Put your hot cock inside me."

He said nothing, but he dipped to her and his swollen cock parted the portals of her vagina. He slid inside, into the warm, velvety inner sanctum of her pussy, and she let out a soft scream of pleasure.

Her hands caressed his shoulder blades as he drove into her, plunging deep into the soft pudding of her cunt. He held her buttocks and lifted them until he pierced the very tip of her vagina and she bucked like a spring colt as an orgasm rippled through her body, one, and then another. Her legs wrapped around his waist and they were a single person, their bodies melded into one thrashing animal exuding sweat and bodily fluids that intermingled like two rivers in a confluence.

He rolled over again until Jasmine was on top and he could see the contours of her face from the dim glow of the streetlamp. She pumped up and down on him, her hair falling over her face like a veil, her arms straight out. She breathed hard and loud as she moved her loins, screwing him into her and thrashing when an orgasm ripped through her body like a firestorm of supreme pleasure.

"Oh, it's so good, John," she said, her voice breathy and low. "You're so good."

"You are some woman, Jasmine," he said. His hands grasped the globes of her breasts and his finger traced the outlines of her nipples until they hardened like tiny buds, pert and stiff as his cock.

The two flipped places again and he stayed deep inside her. She thrashed and squirmed under the energy of his love assault, mewling and purring with pleasure at each thrust and retreat.

"I never . . . I never . . ." she sighed, breathless from the exertion and the ecstatic pleasure.

"Never what?" John asked, a deep huskiness in his voice.

"Never had anything like this. Never felt like this. Never had so much . . . pleasure." The last word out of her mouth was a barely audible whisper that was almost like a prayer on her lips.

"I feel the same," he said, knowing that he could not match her words. There was just no way to describe the way he felt. It was as if he was only half a person and now, with her, he felt whole and complete, as if a lost part of him had returned and given him all that he had ever longed for since childhood.

She was sweet, and her kisses were hot and wet on his face and his mouth. He held his own pleasure back, keeping the seed locked in its pouch so that she could climb to the heights again and again, could soar over the earth like an eagle until she plummeted from the skies into that warm pool of ecstasy that was beyond measure, beyond explanation.

They made love for the better part of an hour. Finally, she let him know that she was ready for the final thrust, that last exquisite moment when all the stars in the sky exploded in her head and flooded her body with warm silver.

"Now, John, now," she urged and he picked up the pace with his thrusting. He dove deep into her loins and her back arched like a Roman bridge, like a ballerina bending backward as her partner grasped her waist and threw her high into the air.

He felt her body relax and then buck as if a spring had been released. He held her tight as the pleasure spewed through his body like warm milk laced with bourbon. He spilled his seed inside her womb and she gripped his shoulder blades like a drowning woman, holding on to him as her own body released all its energy, and sailed to the heights of a mountain where the air was cool and fresh and the breeze like a thousand tongues caressing every inch of her flesh.

"Oh, yes, yes," she sobbed at the height of her ecstasy.

John rose with her to the farthest reaches of the universe, into that godlike realm where all was peace and contentment, weightless as a feather, drained of all energy, but pulsating with an indefinable substance that seemed to fill his mind and caress his body with the hands of an angel.

It was all beauty and harmony as he floated back down to earth, where all was serene and the darkness was like an embrace.

They did not speak for several moments. He tumbled from her and they lay side by side, floating still, even though both were earthbound.

Her breathing returned to normal and so did his, as if they were a matched pair of runners who had just finished a race.

She patted his stomach with a limp hand. But he could feel the calluses on her fingertips. That was her left hand, the one that held the guitar strings down tight between the frets. They were rough, but he loved the feel of them. They were like a badge of her profession, proof that she was a woman who worked, not at washing or ironing clothes, but at something creative and beautiful, which brought joy and happiness to those who heard her play and sing.

"You're a wonder, John Slocum," she said after a time.

"And so are you, Jasmine."

"You got there," she said. "And so did I."

He knew what she meant. They had both gotten there, and they had returned from a holy place denied to most mortals.

"I've never had such pleasure in my life," she said. "Not even singing can match what we had together."

"That's very sweet of you to say so," he said.

"I mean it. I feel safe with you. I feel loved. And that's the greatest feeling in the world."

He said nothing. Just the sound of her soft voice was pleasurable in the aftermath of their lovemaking. Her speaking voice, especially now, was every bit as beautiful as her singing voice. He felt lucky to have been with a woman like Jasmine, a woman who did not demand more than he could give, and gave more than she was given. She was the kind of woman who could grow on a man.

"I think I'll finish the rest of my drink," she said, "and then I've got to go back to my room. Lydia will wonder where I've been."

"Will you tell her?" he asked.

"No, silly. I don't want her to know that her mother is a loose woman."

"You're not a loose woman, Jasmine."

She patted him on his belly, then rose from the bed.

"Thank you for saying that, John. I don't feel loose or immoral. I just feel complete."

"And so do I," he said, marveling once again at the contours of her naked body, the lines and curves that were as classical as a nude painting by a master.

He pulled on his trousers and fished a cheroot from his shirt pocket. He watched her dress, the dainty way she pulled on her pink panties and slid into her cream slip. He lit the cheroot and sat in the darkness at the table.

"You won't light the lamp," she said. "I'm sure I look a fright."

"No, I won't light it," he said. "The darkness looks good on you."

"Mmm," she said, and put on her dress, arranged it as she sat down on the divan. She slipped into her shoes and then drank the rest of her bourbon, a small amount that only covered the bottom of the glass.

"I hope you and the sheriff are successful tomorrow," she said as she stood up to leave.

He walked over to her and took her in his arms.

He kissed her.

She broke away after a few seconds.

"We mustn't do that too much or I'll never get out of here," she said.

"You're beautiful, Jasmine. Inside and out. You're a beautiful woman."

"Oh, you make my poor heart flutter. Good night, John. And good luck."

He walked to the door with her and lifted the wooden latch. He watched her walk down the hall to her room and tap softly on the door. It opened, and a flaring cone of light spilled into the hallway. She stepped gracefully through it and then the door closed and the darkness returned.

John closed the door and latched it. He walked to the window and looked out at the street, over the buildings at the Absarokas, their peaks white and shining in the moonlight.

It was the end of a perfect evening, and tomorrow he and Jenner would go after a man who once had something he never deserved and would never have again.

With luck, Jasmine and Lydia would never have to worry about Bruno Valenti again.

He drew a breath and pulled the shade. He crushed out

his cheroot in an ashtray, pulled the covers back, and slipped into bed. The beauty of the evening was complete and he was tired.

He fell asleep thinking of Jasmine, her aroma still in his nostrils like the fragrance of a fine wine or a lovely rose.

21

Bruno Valenti awoke from a stuporous sleep while silver stars were still winding across the night sky. He had stayed up late, waiting for Angus Macgregor to show up and tell him he had killed the two hunters who had gotten away. He had eaten too much roast lamb, lamb that was not fully cooked, and he had made many trips to the squatting ditch.

The whiskey smell still clung to him and his mouth tasted of rusted copper, his throat raw as a rope burn from too many cigarettes.

"Where in the hell is Macgregor?" he asked aloud and his words bounced off the logs in the small, dingy, rat-shit-infested cabin as if he were talking inside a dank cave.

"Huh?" Jake Pettibone stirred in his bedroll, startled by the booming question. He sat up and opened his eyes. A rat scuttled across the hem of his woolen blanket and made ticking sounds on the log wall with its tiny feet, which were all bone and talons. His vision was blurred, but he could see the watery stars through the openings in the door, the cracks where the wood had weathered and shrunk over the years.

"Get your ass up, Jake," Valenti said. The cigarette in his mouth glowed as he took a puff.

"Hell, it's still night, Bruno."

"Not much it ain't. We got things to do."

"What things?" Pettibone asked, scratching at the lice on his scalp. His eyes still watered as if he'd dunked his head in the creek. The smoke curled through the dark air and assailed his nostrils. He sneezed.

"I want you to be real quiet and go get the other men. Bring 'em back here for a powwow."

"Them Injuns, too?"

"No, just the white men, you stupid bastard. I don't want them Injuns to wake up."

Pettibone tossed his blanket off his body and turned to face the shadowy bulk of Valenti. His hands groped for his boots. He found them and started pulling them on over dirty woolen socks.

"Them redskins drunk enough whiskey, they'll sleep till noon," he said. "Even if you marched through their camp with a brass band."

"They'll sleep longer than that," Valenti said cryptically.

Pettibone was still half-asleep and failed to discern the irony in Valenti's statement. He finished putting on his boots and stood up. His head nearly touched the low roof of the cabin. As it was, he was aware of the nearness and felt claustrophobic.

"Jesus," he said, "who built these cabins? Midgets?"

"Get your ass out of here," Valenti said, and the glow from the cigarette cast a golden shine on his face, a face that made his skin look purple and waxed.

"Yeah, I'm goin', Bruno, just keep your damned britches on, will ya?"

"And don't sass me, Jake. Real quiet, like I said."

The door made a whining noise when he opened it and sagged as it swung out on its worn leather hinges. He closed the door and stared around him, shivering in the chill from a breeze that blew down from the high country like whispers from a glacial cavern.

He walked to the nearest cabin and opened the door. Two men inside snored loudly, out of synchronization, and at different pitches. He walked to one man's hulk on the dirt floor and toed his stockinged foot with his boot. It was Crowley, he knew.

"Wake up, Ben," he whispered as one snore cut off in a loud snort. "Boss wants to see you. Be real quiet."

"Huh? Christ, Jake, you scared the living shit out of me."

"Find yourself a wipe, then, but get on over there pronto."

"What about Harry?"

Harry Wicks snored in his bedroll a few feet away, his bedroll crammed against the wall.

"I'll get his ass up, too, Ben."

"I got to get my boots on," Crowley said. "Hell, it's still night out."

"Yeah, yeah," Jake said. He took a step toward the other sleeper and poked him in the side with the toe of his boot.

"Harry, I'm your morning rooster," Pettibone said. "Cock-a-doodle-do."

Wicks stopped snoring as if a guillotine blade had chopped his head off. He sat up and bumped his head against a log.

"That you, Pettibone?" he whispered, rubbing his head with one hand, his one eye with another.

"Yeah, boss wants us all over at his cabin and he says to be real quiet."

"Now? Shit, it's dark as pitch outside."

"You'll think darker than that if you don't get over there real quick. Bruno's in a foul mood."

"When ain't he?" Wicks said, and crawled out of his bedroll, his blanket rustling like windblown leaves. He pulled on his boots. He and Crowley stumbled from the cabin. Their teeth chattered as they stepped into the predawn chill.

Wicks looked back at Pettibone, who came outside and left their door open.

"Mac get back?" he asked.

"I don't rightly know, Harry. If he did, he'll be bunkin' with Cochran, I reckon."

"Yeah, he will," Crowley said.

Pettibone walked across the dim expanse of flat toward another cabin, his boots squashing grass and grinding pebbles into the dirt. He rubbed his arms against the cold.

The sky was beginning to pale faintly in the east when Pettibone entered the last cabin. There was only one lump on the floor and snores came from beneath the blanket pulled over Jimmy Cochran's head. These were thin, squeaky snores that sounded somewhat like a squealing pig, with whistles at the end of each whining phrase.

Pettibone looked around just to make sure. Macgregor's bedroll was laid out, but it was as flat as a flapjack. Nobody in it.

He toed Cochran in the side once, twice, then put more pressure behind his kick and Jim boiled out of his bedroll like a bass exploding from a quiet pool at the end of a barbed hook.

"Jesus, the Christ," Cochran exclaimed. "What the hell?"

"Get your Irish ass out of bed, Jimmy. Bruno wants to palaver with all of us right quick."

"Now?"

"Yeah, now, goddamn it. And don't make no noise. He don't want to wake them redskins."

Cochran grabbed like a blind man for his boots. He snatched the floppy top of one and dragged it toward him.

"Hell, them Crow was all drunker'n seven hundred dollars last night. A cannon couldn't roust them this mornin'."

"Now, well, just be quiet. Somethin's up and I don't know what."

"Whatta you reckon?"

"I don't reckon, but I don't think Mac got back last night. Look." He pointed to the empty bedroll. "Valenti is plumb pissed off about it."

"Bruno say anything about it?" Cochran pulled on his other boot and grunted from the effort.

"Nope, but I been with him enough to know when somethin's eatin' at him. And when I seen Angus wasn't in his bedroll, I figured that's what's stuck in Bruno's craw."

"Yeah. He was countin' on Mac to drop them two hunters what got away."

Cochran stood up. They left the cabin together and walked across the greensward to Valenti's cabin. There was smoke coming from the tin chimney by then, and they could smell the burning pine. Lantern light shone through the worn-out, moth-eaten burlap that covered the windows.

Pettibone and Cochran entered Valenti's cabin with its thick musk of sweat and stale whiskey mingled with the aroma of burning firewood filling the crowded room with a masculine stench.

"Close the door, Jimmy," Valenti said.

Cochran pulled the door shut and latched it.

"It looks like we lost Angus last night," Valenti said. "He didn't come back and so I figure he either got himself killed or he's lyin' in the timber with a broken back."

"He might have decided to stay in town," Crowley said.

"No, not Mac. I told him to put out the lamps of them two hunters and get right back here. He wouldn't buck me on that."

"Bruno's right," Wicks said in his thin quavery voice. "Mac was a good soldier."

They all looked at Wicks, who seldom spoke out. But they all knew that when he did speak, he had something to say.

"No, something's happened to Mac," Valenti said. "And that means we can't stay here no more. I don't know no place what's got old abandoned cabins, so we might have to sleep under the stars tonight."

There were murmurs and grumblings among the men, but none spoke out to object.

"We've bunked out in the open before," Valenti said, "and it would only be for one night."

"Yeah, but we'll freeze our balls off up here in the mountains," Cochran said.

The men laughed. All but Valenti.

"We might find us some caves along them limestone bluffs," Valenti said. "Either way, we got to get the hell out of this place. If Mac didn't kill them two hunters, and they're still alive, they'll tell the law just where their partner got killed. So we got to light a shuck and be pretty damned quick about it."

"How quick?" Crowley asked.

"As soon as we can pack up. About daylight."

"Well, that shouldn't take long," Cochran said. "We ain't none of us got a whole hell of a lot to pack."

"That's right," Pettibone said.

"Keep your voices down," Valenti said.

They all stopped murmuring among themselves.

"Before we pack out of here," Valenti said, "there's one more thing we have to do."

He let the words sink in. He waited several seconds, his gaze scanning each of their faces.

"What thing?" Pettibone ventured, his voice pitched low and laden with apprehension.

"We got some excess baggage," Valenti said. "Baggage we got to get rid of."

"What baggage?" Crowley asked in all innocence.

Valenti shook a ready-made cigarette out of a pack he had in his pocket. He picked up a shaved stick of kindling, opened the gate of the potbellied stove, stuck it in. When the faggot ignited it, he touched it to his cigarette and pulled smoke into his mouth and lungs.

"The Crow," he said.

Murmurs broke out again. Valenti held up a hand to silence them.

"We don't need 'em no more," he said. "And we can't

just turn 'em loose. We got to kill their red asses, every damned one."

"Jesus," Cochran breathed, and there was a touch of the Irish brogue to the exclamation.

The room went silent again.

Valenti looked at each man and puffed on his cigarette. Crowley pulled a plug of tobacco from his shirt pocket and bit off a chunk. Pettibone shifted his weight from one foot to the other. Wicks seemed to turn pale under the light of the lantern hanging from a hook above him on a ceiling beam. Cochran swallowed and ran fingers through his tousled shock of red hair.

"So, I want you all to get your rifles, real quiet-like, and come back here. We're going to walk over to that Crow camp and surround them teepees. I'll give a whistle when we're all in place. You open up with your Winchesters and Henrys and blow holes in them teepees. Anybody who comes out, we drop him. No mercy. I want it quick and dirty. I want them Injuns to all go to the Happy Hunting Ground before daybreak. Got it?"

The men all nodded and some grunted in assent.

"Be back here in five minutes," Valenti said. "Bring plenty of ammunition. They're aren't many of 'em, but I want 'em all dead."

The men filed out of the room, all but Pettibone. He went to the corner and grabbed his big Henry Yellow Boy. He worked the lever and a cartridge shot into the firing chamber.

Valenti picked up his Winchester '73, and chambered a round. He patted his six-gun and picked up a box of ammunition, stuck several cartridges in his pants and shirt pockets. Pettibone opened a fresh box of ammunition for his rifle and stuffed his pockets full.

In the distance, a crow called, and both men stopped to listen.

"Reckon that bird is a-tryin' to warn them redskins?" Pettibone said.

"It's just a damned bird."

"It's a crow."

"Crow or jay, them Injuns is sleepin'. And I aim to see they don't none of 'em wake up."

The two stepped out of the cabin, into the chill. The sky was filled with stars and there was a fingernail of a moon just above the treetops. It was very quiet. In the distance, they looked at the teepees, all in a circle. No smoke rose from the smoke holes and there was no one on guard.

It was so quiet, they could hear their own breathing, and the squawk of the flying crow died away in the faint glow of the dawn.

22

One by one, Valenti's men all streamed back to where he and Pettibone were waiting. All were armed to the teeth, their jaws set tight and eyes glittering in their sockets like lambent coals on a banked fire. None of the men spoke, but stood with their rifles slung over their shoulders or standing at their sides, butts down.

Valenti counted them without speaking.

Then he nodded and began walking toward the teepees. The men trailed after him in V formation, like geese on the Mississippi Flyway. They tried to walk on the grass and avoid the rocks and gravel. One of the Crow ponies, grazing just inside the timber, lifted its head and whickered softly.

Valenti's face hardened and his lips moved with a silent single-word curse that none could see.

He motioned to some of the men to surround the teepees. He stopped at the entrance to Two Knives' lodge and directed, with a hand signal, for Pettibone to cover the entrance to another teepee.

Then Valenti waited until he no longer heard any foot-

falls. He listened for any sound coming from Two Knives'
lodge. The teepee was as silent as a tomb.

He put two fingers to his mouth, and let out a piercing
whistle.

Then he brought his rifle to his shoulder and fired a shot
through the flap. Explosions boomed from all around the
teepees. A man screamed in pain, one of the Crow.

Valenti moved his barrel and fired again, then levered
another cartridge into the chamber and fired at another place
inside the teepee. He saw something move the entrance flap
and he fired again. He heard a sound like a slap and then a
hard thud as the brave fell back.

The shooting was loud and long.

Some of Valenti's men shouted, and from one teepee came
the sound of a Crow singing his death song. More shots and
the song stopped. Blood seeped from beneath the skins of
some of the teepees.

The guns went silent.

Valenti moved off to his left.

"All right," he shouted. "Now shoot their ponies."

The men walked into the timber and reloaded. They began firing at the paints, and the horses screamed like tor-
tured women. Some of the men wept at the sight of the
slaughter. There were loud thuds and angry whispers, and a
deafening silence afterward.

"Jake," Valenti called out, "you and Jimmy go back to
my cabin and light some wood. Bring the torches back here
and burn down these teepees."

"Ain't you goin' to check to see if we got 'em all?" Pettibone asked.

"We got 'em all. Do it, and do it right now. I want to be
riding out of here before that smoke tells everybody in creation where in hell we are."

"Come on, Jim, let's light some torches," Pettibone said.
The two men took off at a run toward Valenti's cabin.

The other men came out of the timber and stood next to Valenti.

"A hell of a thing," Crowley said.

"It's awful quiet, ain't it?" Wicks said.

"We'll just wait here until Jake and Jim get back and light up these wigwams," Valenti said. "Then we'll all saddle up and ride to the high country."

Wicks stood there, almost invisible, quiet and barely noticeable. His face was expressionless and his eyes as dull as dirty marbles.

"The rifles are plumb hot," Cochran said finally.

"Piss on the barrel," Valenti said.

"Oh, I ain't complainin', Bruno," Cochran said. "I ain't had so much fun since the hogs ate my baby brother."

Nobody laughed at his tired old joke.

Pettibone and Crowley returned with makeshift torches and began to set fire to the hides covering the teepee poles. They went to each one and then tossed the faggots inside two of them.

"All right," Valenti said, "saddle up."

The men walked back to where their horses were hobbled. They gathered them up, saddled them. They brought their bedrolls and saddlebags from their cabins and attached rifle scabbards to their saddles.

When they were all mounted, Valenti pointed to the ridge above them.

He turned and saw the burning teepees. The lodge poles had caught fire and flames rippled up their lengths like some diabolical liquid. The dried hides crackled and fumed. White smoke billowed into the air and was caught by the breeze. Streamers of smoke spread out over the camp and rose above the tall pines in ghostly wisps and patterns.

Valenti turned away and they all rode single file up a game trail to the top of the ridge. They rode in the general direction of Big Timber, but with no destination in mind.

"Whoever comes up to that camp after us," Valenti said to Pettibone, "they ain't goin' to find nothin'."

"I sure hated to shoot them Injun ponies," Crowley said.

"Shut up, Jimmy," Valenti said. "It's over. All of it. We got a bank to rob and a couple of gals to capture."

None of the men spoke from then on. They rode to a place where limestone bluffs broke the skyline and started looking for caves. They saw a she-bear and her cubs off in the distance, and the animals ran up into the timber, their hides glistening and rippling like balled-up water.

The sun appeared on the horizon, yellow as butter, and the trees lit up, their green mantles shining with gold rays gilding the needles. A flock of crows hurtled past them, their cawing calls like the voices of lost children, or as one or two of the men thought, like the ghosts of the dead braves now turning to cinders under a smoky sky.

Valenti found a flat ridge, timbered on three sides, with bluffs protruding from the hillside. There were a couple of small caves and plenty of bear scat and cougar tracks. No sign that any human had been there in centuries.

"We'll make camp here," he said.

He called over Wicks and Cochran, who rode up to him.

He pointed a finger downward and took a map from his saddlebag.

"Somewhere down there is Big Timber," he said. "And somewhere near here, I think the Boulder River has got to be. I want you two to find that river, which cuts right through Big Timber, and find out where Big Timber is, exactly, and mark it on this map."

He made an X on the map with the stub of a pencil he drew from his pocket. He handed the map to Cochran.

"That's where I say we are, where that X is, Jimmy. Now you find me the Boulder and Big Timber. Try to get back by noon."

"All right," Cochran said.

"That river has got to be close, Bruno," Wicks said.

"And you're right. It goes right to Big Timber then runs off into the Yellowstone."

"Okay, then. Find the river and you'll find Big Timber. Don't let nobody see you. You see anybody anywhere near here, you shoot 'em dead, you hear?"

"I got you, boss," Cochran said.

The two men rode off and the others began to make camp. Jake climbed up to one of the caves while Valenti found an open spot in the timber where he could set out his bedroll and have a clear view of the ridge and the bluffs. They had plenty of mutton left and coffee for a week, with sugar and salt and moldy loaves of sourdough bread.

The air warmed under the rays of the sun, and jays flocked to their camp with raucous cries. Chipmunks began to appear on the ledges, and buzzards floated in the sky above their old camp. A thin scrim of smoke hung over that place of death, but the winds were slicing through the streamers and blowing away the gray wisps.

Valenti smiled as he reloaded his Winchester and fished his pack of cigarettes out of his pocket.

All was well, as far as he was concerned, and tomorrow, he would have Jasmine and Lydia under his control.

He smacked his lips in satisfaction and yelled at Crowley to build a fire and make some coffee.

Jake stood on the bluff like some conquering hero, and Valenti beckoned for him to come down.

The smoke from his cigarette scratched at his eyes like shaved onions.

He made a gun of his hand and pointed it at a jay bobbing on a nearby limb. He squeezed the imaginary trigger.

"Bang," he said, and the jay squawked and flew away into the silence of the timber.

23

Slocum was grateful for the coffee Jenner had in his office. He had saddled up Ferro, filled one saddlebag with hardtack, jerky, and a half-dozen cheroots. Jenner, too, was ready to ride once daylight began to dissolve the shadows that filled the streets of Big Timber.

The two men stood outside Jenner's office, steaming cups of coffee in their hands, waiting for the three deputies.

Hoofbeats sounded down the street in the lower part of the town where the Yellowstone ran. Out of the funnel of night rode a lone horseman.

"That would be Cass Lindsey," Jenner said. "He raises horses about five miles out, beyond the river. He lost his young wife about three years ago and lives by himself."

"Mornin', Dave," Lindsey said when he rode up. "I hope you got more of that coffee."

"Light down, Cass. Shake hands with John Slocum then help yourself to a cup inside."

Lindsey dismounted, wrapped his reins around the hitchrail, and shook Slocum's hand.

"Howdy," he said.

"Howdy to you, Cass," Slocum said. Lindsey walked into the sheriff's office, blocking the lamplight for a brief moment. Slocum heard the clank of tin cups as Lindsey poured himself some hot coffee.

Two more riders approached from upper Main Street, the clip-clop of their horses' hooves muffled somewhat by the dirt of the avenue. They passed under the misty cone of gaslight from the streetlamp, their figures distorted like quivering mirages on a desert landscape.

"Here comes the other two deputies," Jenner said. "Jubal Voorhees on the left, on the bay mare, and Luke Chesney on the Appaloosa. They both ride for the Lazy L Ranch west of the Boulder. Feller named Wiggins owns the cattle ranch and he's about as sociable as a tarantula, hardly ever comes to town."

"But he can spare those two men?" Slocum said.

"Calving's over with and the spring gather. They won't brand for another week, so I guess he let those two help me out."

The two men dismounted and tied their horses to the hitchrail. Jenner introduced them to Slocum.

"You like that 'Paloosa?" Slocum asked Chesney.

"Sure. Me'n Jubal left the Lazy L a little after midnight to get here. Speck kept us on the road when it was pitch dark."

"Coffee's inside," Jenner said, and the two men entered the sheriff's office.

Lindsey stood with Slocum and Jenner, blowing the steam off his coffee each time before he drank from his cup.

"Be light soon," he said.

"We'll be riding in dark for a ways," Jenner said. "Soon as those boys finish burnin' their insides."

"How far do we ride?" Lindsey asked.

"Oh, less'n ten mile, I reckon," Jenner said. "Some of it uphill."

"How much uphill?"

"'Bout five mile," Jenner said.

"Whooeee. And how many guns are we facin'?"

"Hard to say," Jenner said guardedly. "Maybe a few arrows."

"Arrows?"

"There are some renegade Crow off the reservation in Wyoming."

"Shit," Lindsey said.

"We have the advantage," Jenner said.

Chesney and Voorhees came out of the office and leaned against the hitchrail, cups in hand.

"How do you figure that, Dave?" Lindsey asked.

"They don't know we're comin' and we have five guns. If we take out five of them with our first shots, why, there can't be more'n one or two left."

"White men or red?"

"White men first. I figure the redskins might light a shuck. Anyways, what I hear is that the Injuns don't have guns."

"I'd hate to have a Crow arrow hit me in the chest," Lindsey said. He drank another swallow of coffee.

"I can get you a skillet to dangle from your neck," Jenner said.

Lindsey laughed.

Fifteen minutes later, the five men rode out of town. They headed east into the washed-out sky of dawn, and by the time they got to the old logging road, the sun was high and bright as a burnished shield of gold. They turned off past the road and climbed the small ridge where the bushwhackers had waited for the coach and wagons that fateful day.

"Lots of tracks," Voorhees said as he scanned the ground. "Some of 'em yours, Dave?"

"Me'n Slocum rode this way up to their camp."

"Notice any new ones comin' down?" Lindsey asked.

"No," Slocum said. "Just ours and theirs. No new ones."

The men were silent after that. Slocum led the way when they neared the old logging camp, but stopped before they rode up to the ridge above the bluffs.

"What's up, John?"

"Smell it?" Slocum said.

All the men sniffed the air.

"Smells like smoke," Lindsey said.

"Wood smoke," from Voorhees.

"Too damned strong for a campfire," Chesney said. "It's all over the timber."

The smell grew stronger as the posse climbed still higher.

Slocum knew something was wrong. It just didn't feel right.

Finally, he stopped again and turned to Jenner.

"You and the others wait here," he said. "I'm going to ride up ahead, flank the camp, and see what made all that smoke."

"All right," Jenner said.

Voorhees and Lindsey rolled cigarettes and lit them. Chesney drank from his canteen. Jenner watched Slocum until he disappeared through the pines and spruce. He listened for any unusual sound.

Slocum approached the camp from the east. He had the idea of coming up behind the teepees he had seen the day before, use them for cover while he scouted the rest of the camp. When he caught sight of a log cabin, he dismounted. He drew his Winchester from its scabbard and ground-tied Ferro to a sapling. He patted his horse on its withers and started sneaking toward the camp.

The smell of wood smoke was strong in his nostrils. He saw something white in the timber near the camp and approached in a low crouch. The closer he got, the more he could see. Paint horses. All unsaddled. All lying dead in a little plot of grass surrounded by tall pines. His stomach turned over and churned.

He crept closer.

He expected to see Crow lodges standing in a circle. Instead, he saw ruins, smoldering ruins, with smoke still spewing from the burned lodge poles and scraps of teepee hides. He saw untouched sheepskins on large willow withes stacked against trees.

Beyond, one of the cabins had its door open, and a thin tendril of smoke rose from its tin chimney.

He stood up straight and looked at the burned lodges.

Skulls and partial skeletons lay strewn among the smoking ashes.

He felt bile rising up his throat and turned away, gulping in a draught of fresh air to keep from vomiting.

"Damn," Slocum breathed.

He waited, looking at all the cabins he could see from his vantage point.

There seemed to be no signs of life. He saw no horses either.

The silence was long and deep.

He felt as if he were looking at a small ghost town. The camp was surely deserted.

What had happened?

He shook his head and walked around the destroyed lodges. There was blood on the ground, drying in the morning sun. Bones and skulls lay in profusion inside the rings where the lodge poles had stood. One skeletal arm reached for the sky, frozen there as if the dying Crow had fallen and struggled to rise when the flames turned him into a cinder.

Slocum swore under his breath.

He walked back to Ferro and untied him. He rode slowly back down to where he had left Jenner and the other men.

Jenner rode out to meet him.

"Well?" he asked.

Slocum didn't say anything until they both reached the other men.

"You don't have to worry about the Crow," Slocum said. "They're all dead. Burnt to a crisp in their lodges."

"What?" Jenner exclaimed.

"Camp's deserted," Slocum said. "It looks like Valenti and his men murdered the Crow while they slept, burned down their teepees, and lit a shuck."

"Shit fire," Jenner said.

"Save matches," Lindsey said without thinking.

The others murmured among themselves.

"Now what?" Voorhees asked as the men went silent.

Jenner looked at Slocum, a questioning look on his face.

"Yeah, John, what now?" he said.

"Valenti's not there. So he has to be somewhere else. Any of you boys trackers?"

"We've all tracked game," Chesney said. "I've hunted with these boys and with Dave."

"Well, we have some tracking to do," Slocum said.

"Maybe they haven't gone," Lindsey said. "Maybe they're lyin' in wait for us in the timber. Hell, they could pick us off like turtles on a log."

"Easy enough to find out," Slocum said. "I have a hunch they went atop that ridge where Dave and I were yesterday and headed toward Big Timber. Valenti wants to kidnap a couple of women and that's where I figured he'd go."

"I think you're right, John," Jenner said. "You lead, we'll follow."

"To make it easy on the rest of you, I'll ride through the camp. You'll be up on the ridge looking down. I'll be the bait. If Valenti and his men are hiding out to bushwhack us, I'll be the first to draw fire. Fair enough?"

"You don't have to do that, Slocum," Voorhees said.

"It'll set your mind at ease. Those outlaws are plumb gone. I can feel it when I look at that camp. They're long gone."

"I hope you're right," Lindsey said.

Slocum fixed him with a hard look.

"We still have to find Valenti, and he won't be easy to catch. Or to kill."

"Why would he murder all those redskins?" Jenner asked.

"I guess," Slocum said, "they weren't useful to him anymore. He's got something he wants to do and didn't want a bunch of renegade Crow hanging on his shirttails."

"Hummm, you might be right."

"Let's go," Slocum said. "No telling how much of a headstart Valenti has on us, but those teepees are still smoking, so he can't have been gone long."

They rode up through the timber. Slocum showed them the camp and the burned Crow lodges. The men, including Jenner, stared at the ruins in disbelief. Lindsey vomited up his coffee. He leaned over from his saddle and just let the liquid erupt from his throat. Then he wiped his mouth.

"You know the way up there, Dave," Slocum said. "I'll ride through the camp and come up on the other side."

"Be careful, John," Jenner said.

Jays hopped around the smoldering teepees and squawked when Slocum rode slowly through the camp, past all the deserted cabins. He found a trail to the upper ridge on the other side and turned Ferro to climb up. At the foot of the bluffs, he stopped. Something caught his eye.

He rode over and looked down at the lifeless body of the other cougar hunter. There were rips in his jacket and shirt and dried blood on his neck. His body was starting to bloat and the smell of death was overpowering.

He rode away from the corpse and began to climb through the timber to the ridge.

The sun shot shafts of light through the pines and the smoke smell was not so bad when he joined the others.

"We found Valenti's tracks," Jenner said. "Jubal's sorting them out. He'll give us a head count in a minute."

Slocum saw that all the men were examining the tracks. Jubal was walking around, counting in his head.

"Five horses," he said.

"Five men," Jenner said.

"And Bruno Valenti's one of them," Slocum said.

Jubal climbed back on his horse. The posse followed the tracks. Each man was wary and they moved slowly along the ridge.

Slocum knew that they could be riding into a trap, an ambush.

He was the wariest of all, for he had ridden that trail many times before.

24

Wicks and Cochran returned less than an hour after they had set out to find the Boulder and the town.

"How far to the river?" Valenti asked.

"'Bout two mile," Cochran said. "As the crow flies."

"How about 'as the horse rides'?" Valenti said sarcastically.

"'Bout the same, Bruno."

"That right, Harry?" Valenti asked.

Wicks nodded.

"Less than two miles, and a rugged ride down to Big Timber. Hard goin'. Lots of brush and the river roarin' in your ears."

"You see the town?" Valenti asked.

"We seen it," Cochran said. "It's about five miles downriver."

"You didn't ride in, though," Valenti said.

Wicks and Cochran both shook their heads.

The others watched as Valenti walked around in a little circle, deep in thought.

Wicks and Cochran dismounted and joined the others.

They sat down, leaned against sturdy pines, smoked and chewed tobacco. They were all in shade, but their bodies were dappled by shadows and streaks of sunlight creased their hats and flickered on their bearded chins.

Finally, Valenti walked back over to them.

"Hell, the town's so close, ain't no need to wait another day. Maybe we won't have to sleep out in the open tonight. We can take that little old bank, grab the two sluts, and find a hotel up in Livingston or Bozeman."

"That sounds right fine with me," Crowley said. "I could use a little extry cash."

The others guffawed at Crowley's crack.

"We ain't more'n an hour from town," Valenti said. "It's Friday and that's when a lot of folks put money in the bank. We can take our time and hit the bank around noon. And we'll have a couple of bitches to keep us company when we ride out of town."

"That sounds like a good idee to me, Bruno," Pettibone said. "I don't much like it up here in this thin air."

"Yeah, you like your air full of cigar smoke and glitter gal perfume," Cochran said.

The others all laughed.

"Mount up, then," Valenti said. "You all know where you're supposed to go and what you're supposed to do."

"Yes, boss," they all chorused.

"Cochran," Valenti said, "you lead the way. Harry, you see he don't stray none."

Wicks nodded. He followed Cochran and they all rode off toward the Boulder River.

Valenti brought up the rear. He kept looking over his shoulder as if to see if they were being followed.

When Pettibone saw what he was doing, he asked Valenti point-blank.

"Why do you keep lookin' over our backtrail, Bruno?"

"I dunno. I got a funny feelin' is all."

"What kind of funny feelin'?"

"Like maybe somebody's on our trail. Maybe we didn't kill all them Crow."

"We kilt 'em all, boss."

"Yeah, I know we did. I just . . ."

He didn't finish his sentence, but Pettibone felt uneasy after that.

Bruno was like a fox. He was smart and he had what he called "instincts." He could smell trouble, and he could sense when somebody was watching or following him.

Pettibone started looking back over his shoulder, too, after that.

When they rode up on the Boulder, the sound blotted out all senses in the men. It was a roaring river at that altitude. It cascaded down over huge boulders and threw up spray filled with tiny rainbows.

Cochran turned to follow the river down toward Big Timber.

Valenti saw that the report was correct, it was rough going, with thick brush, a narrow game trail that petered out every once in a while, then branched off into dense timber.

It might take more than an hour to reach town, Valenti thought. They were riding single file and getting slapped in the face by tree limbs and leaves when the riders in the lead brushed past tall saplings. Down below, Valenti saw the white marred trunks of aspens and the river cutting through flat, rock-strewn ground. He stood up in the stirrups to see if he could see the town, but there was nothing but an old road and more rocks than he had ever seen in his life.

And they were a good quarter to a half hour from getting to the flat.

There, he thought, they would be out in the open.

He stopped looking over his shoulder because he was being whacked by the whip of slender limbs. He raised his arm to keep from being struck in the face. As it was, he had a welt on his forehead and one of his ears hurt as if it had been stung.

"I'll be glad when we're out of this shit," Crowley said.

The other men grunted and forged ahead, hunching over their saddles and hanging on to their hats.

Sunlight speared the dancing waters of the Boulder. It no longer roared, but spoke in loud whispers, winding around huge boulders and sluicing through narrow miniature chasms, spewing blinding white light from its hurtling waters, churning up foam as thick as cream.

To Valenti, it was a long ride down to the flat, and something was itching in his mind, something he couldn't scratch or comprehend.

When they reached the flat and all began to breathe easier, Valenti looked back up the canyon with its impenetrable brush and trees, the gold and silver of the river.

He saw nothing but what was natural to that part of the mountains.

But somewhere, deep in the recesses of his mind, he had a feeling that someone was following him.

And there was that infernal itch in his brain. The itch he could not reach or scratch.

25

Horace Booth, the bank manager, unlocked the outer doors from the inside. He turned around the sign that dangled in the window to read OPEN. The few people who were waiting outside entered the Big Timber Bank & Trust Co.

"Good morning, Mr. Booth," a middle-aged woman said as she passed him.

He smiled and said, "Good morning to you, Mrs. Hutchins."

"Such a lovely day, isn't it?" she said as she walked to a teller's window.

"Perfect," he said, then walked to the door that led to the tellers' cages and his office, pressed a lever to open it, passed through, shut it. The door clicked and was locked. Booth went to his office, where he sat down at his cherrywood desk and began reading the morning paper that had arrived from Billings by stage that morning. He looked at the New York Stock Exchange figures and began writing on a paper pad with a pen from his pseudo-marble inkwell.

Buggies pulled by horses passed in the street. Women with parasols and men in overalls went by the front windows, peering inside at the lines in front of the tellers' windows. Joseph Grant was tending to Mrs. Hutchins, while Carey Newcomb, a prim, pinch-faced woman in her thirties, waited on another customer at the next cage.

Mrs. Adelaide Foreman, a middle-aged widow, sat at her desk outside Booth's office and pecked on one of the new Underwoods recently purchased. She typed very slowly and each strike caused her to twitch with its loud, unfamiliar sound.

Valenti, Cochran, Pettibone, and Crowley rode past the bank and tried to peer through the front window. There were hitch rings and hitchrails in front of all the buildings. The bank was made of red brick and looked imposing next to the buildings made out of lumber. A hardware store and a mercantile store flanked the bank building.

"Looks okay," Pettibone said.

"Yeah," Valenti answered. He turned to talk to Crowley.

"You light down across the street at that flower shop," he said. "Stay by your horse and look both ways. Anybody comes by you don't like, shoot 'em. Especially anybody wearin' a badge. You'll be our lookout."

"Sure, Bruno," Crowley said and turned his horse to cross the street. He waited for a sulky to pass and then stopped in front of Emily's Flower Shoppe and climbed out of the saddle.

"Cochran, you and me are going inside the bank. We'll look things over for a couple of minutes, then you go to one of the tellers' windows. I'll get inside the cage and make the bank president grab money out of the safe. You ready?"

"I'm ready," Cochran said.

"We'll tie our horses up in front of Littlejohn's Hardware Store. One wrap of the reins."

"Got it," Cochran said.

Down the street, Pettibone and Wicks dismounted in front of the Big Timber Hotel. They wrapped their reins around the hitchrail and walked casually up the steps to the porch and entered the building.

They looked around the lobby. Pettibone waited as Wicks walked to the desk and spoke to the clerk.

Alfred Duggins was busy toting up the night's receipts and marking the names and amounts in a small black-and-red ledger. He looked up when the unimposing little man tapped on the counter.

"May I help you, sir?" Duggins asked, a forced smile on his face.

"I'm here to see Jasmine Lorraine," Wicks said. "I have an appointment."

"Is she expecting you?"

"Yes. I'm running a trifle late. If you would just direct me to her room."

"I'll see if she's in," Duggins said, knowing perfectly well that she and Lydia had not come down from their room.

Duggins made a pretext of examining the keys.

"Yes, I believe Mrs. Lorraine is in, but you'll have to see her manager, Mr. Fenster. You'll find him in the dining salon. The waiter will direct you to his table."

"Thank you very much," Wicks said. He looked at Pettibone and walked toward the hallway that led to the dining room.

Pettibone sat down in an overstuffed chair, where he could watch the dining room and the stairway to the second floor.

Duggins went back to his ledger.

He hadn't even noticed the gunman who had come in with the small man asking to see Jasmine Lorraine.

It was a quiet morning and that was the way Duggins liked it.

26

Slocum looked at the moiled ground in the clearing. He saw cigarette papers, mangled and crushed into the dirt. He smelled urine, and there were horse droppings, piss holes in the dirt.

"They waited here for a time," he told Jenner. "Then they rode west, from the looks of those tracks."

"Hell, the Boulder's less than two miles from here. I'll bet that's where they're headed."

Slocum mulled over what Jenner had told him.

"I'll bet they're heading for Big Timber," Slocum said.

"Likely. If they don't know the country, they could just follow the river right into town."

"Is there a quicker way to get to Big Timber?" Slocum asked.

"The Boulder would be rough going. But if we went downslope from here, we could cut out at least an hour's time by not having to fight that brush and those rocks."

"Let's get moving, then. There's no time to waste."

"We'll have to look for a place, but I know the country up here pretty well. Give me a minute."

Jenner rode off through the trees. Slocum and the others waited. They could hear his horse mangling the bushes and saplings. Jenner returned in less than three minutes.

"Follow me," he said. "We'll have to follow a switchback game trail, but it leads right down to the flat. There's a road there that intersects the one leading into town."

Slocum nodded. He and the others followed Jenner through thick brush and then saw the game trail zigzagging down the slope. It was narrow, so they all rode single file. They reached the bottom in less than ten minutes. Jenner turned on the rutted road and headed west.

They crossed over a log bridge that spanned the Boulder River and turned on the road to Big Timber.

"How far to town?" Slocum asked.

"I don't know exactly," Jenner said. "Maybe four or five miles."

"Let's run a race," Slocum said. He turned to the other men. "We'll gallop a mile or so, then trot for a mile. Can you keep up?"

"We can keep up," Jubal said.

Slocum put Ferro into a gallop. Jenner came right up beside him, grinning as he hunched over his saddle horn like a jockey.

A half hour later, they rode past Velva's place and headed down Main Street toward the hotel.

Slocum saw the two horses tied up at the hitchrail and his heart sank.

He recognized the brand. Those were horses he had sold to Valenti.

Then, as they rode up to the hotel, he glanced down the street.

There, in front of the bank, he saw two more horses that he recognized.

He turned to Jenner.

"There are two of Valenti's men inside the hotel," he said. "Don't ask questions, but I see two more horses I sold him down at the bank. I'll take Jubal in with me, and you'd better hightail it down to the bank. Something's sure as hell up."

"Damn," Jenner said. He turned to the other two men, Luke Chesney and Cass Lindsey. "Follow me," he said, "and be ready to shoot."

"Jubal, you come with me," Slocum said. They tied their horses at the hitchrail.

"What's up?" Jubal asked as they climbed the steps.

"I think there are two men in here who are trying to kidnap the Lorraines."

"Who are the Lorraines?"

"Never mind. Just be ready to shoot if you see anybody with a gun who looks like he might kill you."

"Jesus," Jubal said, and wrapped his fingers around the butt of his pistol.

Slocum pushed the door open and strode into the lobby.

Duggins staggered out from behind the desk, holding a hand to his bleeding head. He pointed to the stairs then pitched forward and fell to the floor with a thud.

At the top of the stairs, Slocum saw a terrified Fenster braced by two men. He looked at Slocum with wild eyes, and then was gone, pushed ahead by the larger of the two men.

"Watch yourself, Jubal," Slocum said, and started climbing the stairs.

Slocum heard someone pounding on a door. A moment later, he heard a crash, then a woman screamed.

Heavy footsteps sounded down the hall. Then another woman screamed.

A man yelled something that Slocum couldn't understand.

Then, as he reached the top of the stairs, he heard a gunshot. A loud gunshot. Then there was a heavy thud and more screaming from two women.

He ran down the hall, Jubal at his heels, and saw the

open door. He saw a body lying on the floor in the doorway, but couldn't see who it was.

More male voices. More screaming. Then he heard another shot, not as loud as the first, and his heart stopped. He knew what it was that he had heard.

It was a Derringer.

Jasmine's hideout pistol.

And then Lydia screamed at the top of her voice.

27

Jenner noticed the brands of the two horses and that they were the same as those on the horses in front of the hotel.

Slocum didn't miss much, he thought.

As they neared the bank, he saw the man across the street in front of the flower shop. He was standing by his horse, pretending to adjust his stirrups. But the man was out of place.

As a lawman, Jenner had learned to read people, especially suspicious people like this man. As he rode closer, he recognized him as one of Valenti's men, a man he had seen at the old loggers' camp with the other outlaws.

He didn't know the man's name, but that didn't matter now. There were two men at the hotel, one in front of the flower shop, and probably two more inside the bank.

He turned to Chesney and Lindsey.

"Cass, you and Luke go to the bank and cock your rifles. You see anybody run out with money bags, you throw down on 'em."

"What?" Chesney said.

"Don't ask questions. Two men are robbing the bank. I'm going over to the lookout across the street."

"Holy Christ," Lindsey said, and pulled his rifle from his boot.

Jenner angled his horse toward the man in front of the flower shop.

Crowley saw the man pull his rifle and reached for his pistol.

"Hold it right there," Jenner yelled. He drew his own pistol.

Chesney pulled his rifle from its scabbard and levered a round into the firing chamber.

Crowley cleared leather and started to swing his pistol toward Jenner.

Jenner dug his spurs into his horse's flanks and yelled. The animal leaped forward, heading straight for Crowley.

Jenner fired as he ducked, hugging his horse's neck, Indian-style.

Crowley fired at him. The shot went wild and Jenner reined up a few feet from him.

"Drop it," he told Crowley.

"Fuck you," Crowley said and swung his pistol to take aim at Jenner.

Jenner straightened his arm, sighted down the barrel until he had Crowley's head square in his sights, and squeezed the trigger.

Crowley's facial expression went blank as a hole appeared in the middle of his forehead. The back of his skull blew off in a spray of rosy blood and bloody oatmeal. The skull crashed into the window of the flower shop and cracked the pane on the window.

Crowley's legs turned to jelly and he collapsed in a heap. His pistol slipped from his fingers. Women on the street screamed and men dove into doorways for cover.

Just then, the bank doors opened and two men came running out.

Jenner recognized them.

Valenti and Cochran.

Lindsey yelled, "Stop," and brought his rifle to his shoulder.

Valenti fired at Lindsey's horse at point-blank range. His bullet struck the animal in the chest and it staggered backward as its front legs crumpled. Lindsey flew out of the saddle.

Cochran fired his pistol at Chesney, who screamed as the bullet slammed into his arm above the elbow. His rifle fell from his hands and clattered on the ground.

"Halt!" Jenner cried.

Cochran threw a shot in his direction. Jenner ducked and heard the bullet whine over his head. He fired at Cochran, but out of the corner of his eye, he saw Valenti scampering down the street toward the hotel. He swung to get a shot, but Cochran got to his horse, stuffed a bag in his saddlebag, and fired another shot at Jenner. The bullet whistled past Jenner's ear and he saw Cochran mount up, wheel his horse toward Chesney, and run him down. Cochran's horse crashed into the Appaloosa and Chesney went flying, his rifle turning somersaults in the air.

Jenner twisted his horse into a tight turn and went after Cochran, who was racing toward the hotel.

There was no catching him, Jenner knew. He stopped, cocked his pistol, took aim calmly, and fired at Cochran's back. He saw the man stiffen. His back arched and he turned in the saddle to look at Jenner.

Blood spewed from a hole in his back and he dropped his pistol and hung on to his saddle horn with both hands. His horse galloped a few yards before Cochran fell sideways out of the saddle and landed in a heap on the ground.

Jenner looked over at the hotel.

Valenti had disappeared.

28

Slocum stepped over the body of Fenster into a scene of pure horror.

Wicks was slumped in a chair holding his belly. Blood seeped through his fingers. He had a dazed look on his face, and his eyes were fixed and glazed.

Jasmine lay on the floor, blood streaming from a cut in her scalp. Her locks dripped crimson droplets onto her chemise.

Pettibone had his arm around Lydia's neck and was squeezing her so tight, her lips had turned blue, her eyes were rolled back so that only the whites showed, and she appeared to be going into a swoon.

Slocum pointed his Colt at Pettibone.

"Let her go, you bastard," he said.

Pettibone wheeled so that Lydia was in the line of fire.

"Back on out of here, buster, or you'll join shithead there on the floor."

Lydia slumped and her eyes closed. She was deadweight on Pettibone's arm.

Slocum held his pistol waist high, his thumb on the

hammer. Pettibone stuck his pistol in front of him, next to Lydia's limp arm. The barrel pointed directly at Slocum's middle.

Jasmine moaned and stirred.

Wicks made a noise in his throat.

He groaned in pain and looked at Slocum with glassy eyes that seemed fixed on a point beyond Slocum, somewhere in space, perhaps someplace in eternity.

"You got me," Slocum said. He eased the hammer down on his Colt and slipped it back in his holster. He held his hands up in a sign of surrender.

"That's better," Pettibone said. He released his grip on Lydia and she slid, slumping, to the floor.

"Now, back on out of here, mister," Pettibone said, "and don't look back."

Slocum glanced down at Jasmine. Her Derringer lay a foot away from her hand and she was still bleeding from her scalp.

"You heard me," Pettibone said. "Get movin'."

Slocum backed toward the door. He turned to go out and dropped his hands. He reached into his belt and pulled out his Remington belly pistol. As he reached the door, he wheeled and cocked the pistol, fired at Pettibone.

Pettibone's face registered surprise as the lead ball slammed into his gut. He staggered backward. Slocum shifted the belly gun to his left hand, drew his Colt, thumbed the hammer back, and fired at Pettibone again. Pettibone's chest caved in from the impact of the bullet and a fountain of blood spurted from his breastbone. He took two steps backward and fell flat on his back, sucking blood into his lungs instead of air. He made a gurgling sound in his throat.

Slocum heard a rustling and turned to see Wicks raising his pistol to aim it at Jasmine.

Jasmine's eyes fluttered and she saw the barrel of Wicks's pistol a few feet from her face. Her mouth opened and she let out a piercing scream.

Lydia came to at that instant. She had a bewildered look on her face as she touched her fingers to her bruised throat.

Slocum swung his pistol fast, hammering back. Just as Wicks was about to squeeze the trigger on his gun, Slocum fired at the little man's head from a foot away. The bullet struck Wicks in the ear and blew through the other side of his head. Brain matter smacked into the wall.

Lydia screamed in terror.

Jasmine gasped and struggled to sit up.

Wicks toppled over, blood gushing from his ear and from the other side of his head. His pistol hit the floor with a dull thump.

"Look out," Lydia screamed, and Slocum wheeled. There, in the doorway, was Valenti, a murderous look in his eyes, a pistol in his hand.

Slocum had just a split second to think and he pulled the hammer back to full cock, held his breath, and squeezed the hair trigger. The Colt boomed with a roar that resounded in the room and down the hall.

Valenti snarled as the bullet struck him in the midriff, and he swung his pistol on Jasmine.

She groped for her Derringer, grabbed it up. She pointed it at Valenti as she pulled one hammer back. The lower barrel spouted flame and sparks, and the pistol cracked like a bullwhip. Her bullet caught Valenti in the chest and ripped through his heart. His hand went limp and his pistol dropped from his hand.

"Bitch," he murmured with his last breath before he fell over dead, atop the lifeless body of Fenster.

Smoke hung in the air like coils of white cobwebs.

Jenner burst through the door, gun in hand, stepping over the two bodies.

He looked at Slocum and then at the two women. Then he saw the body of Pettibone lying near the bed and the back window.

"You all right?" he asked Slocum and the two women.

"We're just fine," Jasmine said.

She got up and put her arms around Lydia. "Aren't we, honey?"

"Yes, Ma, we're fine."

Jenner holstered his pistol.

"You know something, John?" he said. "There ain't nobody left to arrest. I shot Cochran outside the hotel and it looks like you took care of Valenti and a couple of others."

"Jasmine took Bruno down," Slocum said softly. "She's quite a shot."

Jasmine looked up at Slocum. Then she and Lydia rushed over to him and wrapped their arms around him.

"You're my hero," Jasmine whispered.

Lydia looked up at Slocum with desire in her eyes.

"Mine, too," she said, and gave him a squeeze that left no doubt in his mind that she would grace his bed one night soon, just like her mother.

The acrid smell of gunsmoke drifted through the open window and a fresh breeze ruffled the curtains.

Jasmine's head had stopped bleeding and the color had returned to Lydia's cheeks.

Slocum pulled out a cheroot and stuck it in his mouth.

"Buy you a drink, Dave," he said to Jenner.

"I'll buy you one," Jenner said. "Hell, I'll buy everyone a drink."

Lydia and Jasmine laughed.

"Then I won't say I've got a headache," Jasmine said.

Slocum's chest swelled as he took a deep breath and looked at Jasmine with intense admiration.

Yes, she could grow on a man. She was a woman to ride the river with, all right.

Watch for

SLOCUM AND THE COW CAMP KILLERS

390th novel in the exciting SLOCUM series
from Jove

Coming in August!